Captive Shadows

Written by: Emily Klepp
Edited by: Amanda Austin,
Jade Katzchen, Brittany Slater
Cover art by: Juniper Meadows

Cover design by: Juniper Meadows

*To all the those who find it in themselves to forgive
the unforgivable and irredeemable…*

Captive Shadows

For twenty-five years, all I have known is pain. I've endured the worst that someone could do to another human. One day I took a leap of faith, only to be caught and cared for. I thought the jump was the hardest part until family secrets threaten my freedom and newfound happiness. When enemies become family and friends become lovers, anything can go wrong. Love, growth, and new connections will only get me so close to freedom before I have to crawl out alone. Will I survive the collapse of an empire or will I burn in the rubble of my family's affairs?

This is a DARK romance novel with MASSIVE triggers. Maya endures major trauma but does get her HEA. Her story is not for the faint of heart and caution is highly advised. Please read the trigger warnings before proceeding with her story.

Tropes: Age gap, Polyamorous/MFFM, Bi-Awakening, healing, Instalove, Breeding (with result), Brat, pleasure dom, Voyeurism, exhibitionism, revenge, HEA, Mental health rep, Touch her and die vibes, protective MMCs,

Triggers: Sexual assault, Domestic violence, Self-harm, suicidal ideation, Eating disorder, Incest, Kidnapping, Murder, attempted, unwilling at-home abortion.

Russian translations:

Igrushka (Игрушка) = Toy

Dochka (Дочка) = Daughter

Chapter One

Maya

I hate working at this fucking bar. All it does is cause Jonathan and me to fight before I go to work. Although if it wasn't this, he would just find something else to call me a cheating whore over. For the record, I have never cheated. No matter what he says or does, I will never stoop as low as him. My staying with him after catching him cheating does make me a dumbass, though. I know what to expect from him. I know that every few months I'll come home from work to find him with his dick in some girl in our bed. He always finds a way to blame me and says that I don't put out so therefore he has to find pussy on his own. That doesn't stop him from forcefully fucking my throat when he gets mad at me. It's like a power move to show me who's in control.

There is an entire world wide web full of porn that he can jerk off to. Why does he have to go stick his dick in everything with a heartbeat? Then he wonders why I don't want to sleep with him. If I wanted to catch a disease, I'd fuck one of the many customers who grope or fawn over me every night.

When I first got with Jonathan, he would tell me that men looked at me that way because I was beautiful. Now, he would tell me it's because I am a trashy whore who begs for attention from anyone who will look at me.

I used to have a stellar level of self-confidence. Before, I'd never look in the mirror and been disgusted with my body but now, here we are. I am staring at myself and I want to think I am beautiful, but his constant insults play on a loop in my head.

"Your thighs are too big. Maybe you should diet? You look like trash in that. No one wants to see all of that fat. Maybe baggier clothes would hide your rolls better. Your stretch marks look gross."

The list goes on and on. If it's something that can be thought of, he has said it to me. I am five foot three on a good day. I carry all of my weight in my thighs and ass, but my stomach is what makes me cringe the most. I have tried every diet and exercise you can think of but the only thing that helps is simply not eating. I exercise every morning when I get off work and I don't eat unless I have to. Generally, that is one small meal a day so I don't pass out at the gym again.

I pull my long dark brown hair up into a high ponytail before getting dressed. Naturally, Jonathan forgot to do laundry again so I am stuck with short shorts and a snug-fitting purple shirt. It's incredibly low cut, but that will only help me with tips tonight. Las Vegas in the summer is especially miserable, so the small amount of clothing I am wearing will ensure I don't have a heat stroke.

"There is no fucking way you are wearing that to work," Jonathan snaps at me as he walks into the bedroom.

Jonathan is a year older than I am, at twenty-five. He looks like your stereotypical fuck boy, but his fish lips ruin his face. Above all, he looks like he *should* be handsome, but something about him is off. Maybe it's his arrogance or maybe it's his sour attitude, but it makes him ugly when he is so fucking cruel to me. And to think that I once thought he was my happily ever after.

"I wouldn't have to if you had done laundry like I asked you to," I retort. Maybe I shouldn't be smarting off to him when he's already in a bad mood.

"Don't fucking blame me. You had every opportunity to get off your fat ass this morning and do it yourself," he says as he walks closer to me.

"I worked a double yesterday and you have yet to find a fucking job. The least you could do is wash the fucking clothes," I huff. Yeah... This is going to go wonderfully.

"Your clothes. Your problem. Don't put your shit off on me."

"I'll remember that the next time you want something from me," I mumble as I turn to grab my bag.

"*What the fuck did you just say to me?*" he screams at me as he shoves me backward. My back hits the floor-length mirror and it shatters, cutting the back of my arm.

"*God damnit, Jonathan,*" I scream at him. I grab the shirt I was just wearing and press it to my arm before it gets on my only clean shirt. I already know that I'm going to pay for smarting off to him. This is only the beginning. The screaming at him ensures that he's going to forcefully face fuck me again.

Jonathan gets in my face, ignoring that he just cut my arm open. "I swear to fucking god, If I catch you flirting with one motherfucker in that bar, I'll fucking kill you," he says in a grave tone.

"Okay," I say in a quiet voice. I know when to keep my mouth shut. The last thing I want to do is spend the next two weeks covering up a bruise because he hit me again. I've gotten by with no one noticing, but someone is bound to catch on that I'm a fucking idiot and refuse to leave the man who threatens to kill me every time he hurts me.

"Now apologize for breaking my mirror," he says as he grabs my face.

"I-I'm sorry," I whimper as pain floods my face from how he grips my chin.

"Get on your fucking knees and show me how much, Maya," he says with a sickening smirk.

"Jonathan, I need to go to work," I say quietly.

"You'll go to work when I tell you to go to work," he says as he shoves me to my knees and pulls his dick out. "Now open your mouth."

I sigh heavily and do as he tells me to. He grabs the sides of my face and forces himself down my throat. I am so accustomed to this level of force from him that I no longer have a gag reflex. Lucky for me, he never lasts long. He may be hung but he never spends more than a few minutes fucking my face before he groans obnoxiously loud and comes. He always pushes down my throat when he comes so that I am forced to swallow. That wretched taste is what makes me gag.

"Go to work and remember what I said," he says as he steps away from me and leaves the room.

I pick myself up and go to the bathroom to look at my arm. Thankfully, I didn't get any blood on my shirt. I clean it up the best I can before putting a bandage on it. Jonathan finding some way to make me bleed is going to cause me to have to buy stock in bandages.

For the first time, I find the bravery to want to leave him. I could work one last shift, take the cash, and run. I have no family and he's isolated me away from my old friends. I have nothing tying me to this fucking town. Before I can talk myself out of it, I go to the safe and grab my important papers like my social security card and birth certificate. I shove them in my bag before Jonathan catches me.

He thinks he has me scared enough to never run from him, but he doesn't have the first clue what I will do. I'm not scared of him, I'm scared of running and being alone. I have no one and he knows it. I've gotten to the point where I'd rather be alone than for him to constantly be hurting me. Who needs self-harm when you have a psychotic boyfriend who will do it for you? My skin is littered with tattoos to cover the scars that he and I have caused to my body.

Something has to change because I am tired of the bloody bandages. I'm tired of making excuses for injuries. What kind of fucking monster cuts his own girlfriend as punishment? Oh right... Jonathan.

I grab whatever I can reasonably shove into my bag before grabbing my keys and going to the door. "I need $400 by tomorrow so you better do well tonight," Jonathan says as he cracks his piss water beer open.

"Okay," I say simply. "I'll text you when I leave." I get out of the house before he has a chance to stop me and jog to my car.

My car is a piece of shit and it won't get me far, but I'll take her as far as she lets me go. After that, I'll get on a bus and keep going. Once I hit the East Coast, I'll pick the smallest town I can find and hide out.

As I drive to work I get excited about the possibility of finally being free. I get inside and put on my apron before clocking in.

"Hey, Maya," Elliot says. Elliot Greene is the bar

owner. He owns more than a dozen across the city and comes in for a shift once a week. He's always here for my weekend shift. It's the one day a week I look forward to.

Elliot is a rugged-looking man, but drool-worthy nonetheless. He stands well over a foot taller than me and has a dark, neatly styled beard. He's the perfect mixture of a lumberjack and a biker. Every time he's here, he brings his Harley.

"Hey," I say with a smile.

"What happened to your arm?" he asks, gesturing at my bandage.

"Oh… I wasn't paying attention and fell back into a mirror in my room," I lie.

"You're bleeding through it," he says as he takes my arm.

"Ah, fuck," I sigh.

"We have a few minutes. Let me clean it up," he says. "Fiona, grab the first aid kit, please."

"Woah. What happened?" she asks.

"A mirror attacked me," I say. She gives me a weird look, knowing I'm lying. She's the only person who's gotten closest to putting the pieces together.

Fiona grabs the kit and brings it to Elliot before greeting the early drinkers who walked in. "This is pretty deep," he says as he takes the bandage off of my arm.

"Glass has that effect on the skin sometimes," I say.

"Smart ass," he says with a chuckle. "It doesn't need stitches."

"That's good, I suppose."

"I made some fries," Richard says. "You want some Maya?"

"I'm good. I ate before I came in," I lie. "Thanks though."

"There ya go," Elliot says as he places another bandage on my arm. "Stay away from the mirrors."

"Too soon, Elliot. Too soon," I say and he laughs.

I go behind the bar and greet Stephen. He comes in here every night before going home to his wife. That should be repulsive, but he tips well and he doesn't grab my ass, so it's a win in my book.

I stay busy all night. I don't think I stop running for more than a minute at a time, and that's just to make drinks. Every seat in the building is taken up until I make last call. The cooks leave first, then Fiona. I am sitting at the bar counting my cash tips when I hear Jonathan's car pull up. I have just over three hundred in cash. He's going to be so fucking mad. I have no idea what I have on credit, but he won't care to wait. He will get pissed right away.

I jump up right as he walks in. "I thought you said you'd text?" he asks.

"I'm not done yet. I won't be leaving for at least another hour," I say. I try to move away from him but he pushes me back up against the bar and takes the money out of my hand. Thank god Elliot is in his office or this would get ugly fast.

"I still need to count the credit tips," I say.

"This isn't four hundred," he says as he puts the money in his pocket. "You are more than fifty short."

"I know. I said I still need to count..." My words are cut off when he slaps me across the face. I am too stunned to say or do anything, so I just stand there.

"I'll deal with you at home," he growls at me before turning on his heels and leaving with all of my cash.

"What was that?" Elliot asks as he comes out.

"Nothing," I say. I stay facing away from him because I know I have a handprint on my face again. I move to the register to cash out and Elliot grabs my arms and turns me around.

"Who the fuck hit you?" he says when he sees my face. He lifts my chin to the light to get a betting look at me.

"Jonathan," I say tearfully. He closes his eyes and takes a deep breath.

"I know you're getting hurt all of the time by him, Maya. You need to leave him," he says.

"I'm trying. I have all of my papers. I just have to figure a few things out first," I say. "I promise I'm trying."

"What can I do?" he asks.

"Can you hold onto my social and birth certificate? If he knows I got a hold of them, he will destroy them," I say.

"Yeah. I'll put them in the safe," he says. I grab my bag out from under the bar and hand him the papers. "Come here." He gestures for me to walk with him to the office. I watch as he unlocks the safe and places my paperwork inside. Before he shuts it, he pulls out a flip phone.

"What's that for?" I ask.

"You," he says simply. "Hide it and call me day or night. My contact is already in it."

"You don't have to do this. I'll be.."

"My sister was killed by her boyfriend because she didn't have a way to reach anyone. Take the phone and call me day or night, okay? I learned with her that you can't force someone to leave because they will end up going right back to them. I know you need to do this in your own time, but I want you to have a backup plan if he escalates more."

"Alright," I say as he places the phone in my hand.

"It's fully charged. Just charge it while you are here so you don't have to worry about doing it at home," he says. "Why was he mad?"

"He wanted $400 and my cash tips weren't enough," I say.

"You've done over $200 on credit though?" he questions. "Just take him the rest of what he wants and leave the rest of the cash here. Keep adding to it so you have some savings."

"Thank you," I say quietly. "I'm sorry about your sister."

"No need to apologize. I missed the signs and let her down. That's on no one but me," he says. "Get out of here and I'll finish closing up."

We walk back to the bar and cash out. I take seventy so that he's not suspicious of me only getting $400 for the night. The rest I give to Elliot to put in the safe before I grab my stuff and go to the car.

I don't want to go home yet. I know it's going to be bad. I need to buy myself some more time though. He is likely tracking my phone right now so I know I won't get far if I run now. I text Jonathan as promised before driving back toward the house.

When I get home, he is sitting on the couch drinking. "Get me the rest of my money?" he asks, glancing at me.

"Yes. I had seventy on credit tips," I say as I hand him the cash. Instead of taking the cash, he stands up.

Fuck. He's going right for it this time. I have the flip phone turned off and in my bra so in the worst-case scenario, I'll hide and call Elliot if he gets too violent.

"What do I have to do to get you to listen to me the first time I say something?" he asks as he backs me down the hallway.

"I did listen. I got you what you wanted," I say.

"After I had to go all the way up to your work. What did you do, fuck your boss for extra cash?"

"What? No. I just hadn't cashed out when you got there. I would have done it sooner if I..." He cuts off my words again by slapping me. This time I fall to the ground. He promptly grabs me by the hair and drags me up to bend over the bed. He pins me with his hand between my shoulder blades as he jerks my shorts down. "*Stop it*," I yell at him as I try to get up.

"Is this what it will take to get you to listen?" he slurs. There's no telling how long he's been drinking. He's never done this. He's never forced himself on me like this. "So I need to fuck you to get you to listen?"

"*Jon, stop. Please stop it*," I scream. "*I'll listen. I promise I'll listen.*"

"I think this is exactly what you want, Maya. I think you want me to fuck you. I think you push and push and push so I would break and fuck your fat ass," he says.

"No. I don't. Please stop it," I beg as I start crying.

With nothing else for him to say, he shoves himself inside of me. I let out a blood-curdling scream as he starts to violently fuck me. I can't get any words out past my screams as he keeps pounding into me over and over. The seconds feel like minutes and I wish he would finish already. Alcohol always makes him last longer and I fucking hate it. At least with him throat fucking me it doesn't hurt. This is agonizingly painful. There is no way I'm getting away from this without injury.

With a loud groan, he thrusts once more before pulling out of me and coming. When I feel his fluids hit my lower back as he finishes himself off, I start sobbing.

He steps away from me and I move to sit on the ground.

"Worthless cunt," he says as he spits on me. He turns and leaves the room, slamming the door behind him. When I hear the lock on the outside of the door engages, I know I need to find a way out of this house. He only locks that door if he plans on keeping me in here for a while.

I focus on cleaning up first, so I go to the bathroom and wash him and the blood off me as best as possible. Luckily, I don't think he hurt me too badly. I'm going to be sore for a while though.

I sit on the bed and wait a while before taking the chance to turn on the phone. I don't know if it makes sounds when it comes on, so I put a pillow over it as I press the power button. This trailer is small enough that he would hear it if it went off. I'm sure he's passed out drunk by now though.

I lock myself in the bathroom before going to Elliot's contact and calling him. I don't want to bring him into this, but it's my only option.

The second I hear his voice, I start crying again. "Maya. What happened?" he asks hurriedly.

"He has me locked in the bedroom," I say tearfully.

"Did he hurt you?" he asks.

"Yeah. I don't know how to get out. I need to leave. I don't know what to do," I cry.

"Take a deep breath. Do you still live in that trailer on Willow?" he asks.

"Yeah. The brown one."

"Okay. I'm on my way. What end of the house are you at?" he asks.

"I'm in the room on the far end by the woods. It's too far to jump." I say.

"I'll be there to catch you. I promise. I need you to gather what you can but don't make any unnecessary noises. Okay?"

"Are you going to stay on the phone?" I ask.

"I'm not going anywhere. I promise," he says. "I just left the bar, so I'm not far."

"He came after me the second I walked in," I say.

"What did he do?" he asks.

"He slapped me again and he... Uhhh.... I think he raped me," I say quietly.

"Oh, Maya... I'm so sorry" he sighs. "I'm just around the corner. Go ahead and open the window." I run to the window and quietly open it up. When I see him outside the window, I close the phone and put it in my pocket.

"So I just jump?" I ask quietly.

"Yeah. Put your feet out first, then your body. I'll catch you," he says. I hear movement in the house and my eyes go wide. "Maya, come on sweetie. I'm right here."

I carefully get out of the window and right as I jump, the bedroom door comes open. Elliot catches me then takes my hand and drags me out of the view of the window. We pass by a few trailers before crossing someone's yard to get to Elliot's bike.

"It's a little big, but it's better than nothing," he says as he puts his helmet on me.

"Thank you," I say quietly.

"You're welcome, Maya. Let's go before he comes looking for you," he says as he gets on the bike. I get on behind him and he pulls my arms forward to wrap around him. "You've got to hang on."

I hear Jonathan's loud ass car roar to life and I gasp. "Elliot, that's him. He's coming," I say hurriedly.

"Hang on," he says as he starts his bike and starts

down the road. As soon as we hit the main road he takes off.

Elliot easily could have come into that house and kicked his ass and left with me, but it would have made everything worse. He could have killed Jonathan, but then I really would be alone. He has likely suspected that I've been abused for a while. He seems pretty prepared with that phone as if he was just waiting for me to open up to him. He's the only one that I know wouldn't be dramatic about it. There doesn't need to be this huge fanfare over me being abused. It happened, it is over, I just need to move on. Sitting here dwelling on it or feeling sorry for myself is not going to do anything that causes me more mental strain. Maybe other people like to sit and hash out their feelings, but I don't. Maybe it's from having a lifetime of disappointment.

We pull into his driveway and get off the bike. He walks his bike into the garage, and then takes his helmet from me. "We can go in the morning and get the cash and papers from the bar," he says.

"Oh, right. Thank you," I sigh. "I don't know what to do now. I have nowhere to go. I don't have my car and like fuck if I'm going back for it. He can keep everything for all I care. I can get new stuff. That means I need to buy new clothes though. If I went back into that house, even if just to get my stuff, he would do far worse than he already did before. I'm lucky that's all he did considering..." I abruptly stop talking.

"Let's go inside, okay?" he says softly and I nod.

When we get inside I suddenly feel trapped again being inside. It feels like the walls are closing in on me. The feeling is constricting my chest, making it hard to breathe. I can feel the panic swelling inside of me.

He's looking at me like it's the most normal thing to be happening. He simply leads me to the couch to sit down. When I start to hyperventilate he rubs my back while I focus on taking slower breaths.

He didn't spew the bullshit about how everything was going to be okay and how I'm safe now. Even he knows that it is a lie. Jonathan could come after me at any moment, and he likely will. Running and staying in this town only has consequences. The benefit of living in Las Vegas is the fact that there are over 600,000 residents and countless tourists. As long as I stay the fuck away from anywhere, I went before, I should be able to avoid him until I can figure out how to leave.

"I can't be here," I say when I start to calm down.

"Why?" he asks.

"All I'm doing is putting you in his crosshairs. He is cruel and he doesn't give a fuck about anybody but himself. Me being here will only get you hurt," I say.

"Let me worry about me," he says simply. "I wouldn't have brought you here if I thought I couldn't handle it."

"I... I will leave as soon as I can. I don't want to intrude on your life. I know you want to help, but that doesn't mean that you should have to sacrifice shit for me. I have a plan to get to the coast. I was going to use the money from tonight before he took it. That could've gotten me gas until my car gave up, but now I don't even have a car. I suppose I could still take a bus. For all I know, he tracks my car. Maybe it would be better to just leave everything behind, including the car. It's in my name, but I don't really give a shit anymore. I'm just sick of getting hurt over stupid shit. At least if I get hurt it's my fault."

"Maya," he says softly.

"I'm sorry. I'm rambling," I say with a sigh.

"That's not what I'm talking about. You can vent all you want, but understand you can be here for as long as you need to," he says.

"I have a little cash. I can get a hotel room and just work until I have enough saved to go somewhere else," I say.

"First of all, no. You're not staying in a hotel. Also, I don't think you should return to the bar," he says.

"What? Why? I promise there won't be any more problems," I start to say but he puts his hand up to stop me.

"Maya, honey. He knows where you work," he says. "The first thing he will do is come to that bar tomorrow and see if you're there."

"Yeah," I sigh. Elliot is right. He'd show up and drag me back to the house. For who knows what he'd do to me there. "I need to work. I need to have money. Without money, I may as well just go back because I can't survive on my own without money."

"Slow down, Maya. I need help at the office, so just come help me with paperwork. You'll get paid more that way anyhow," he says. "Despite what you may think, I do want you here. You are not a burden."

"I feel like a burden. I feel like I'm coming into your life and wrecking it. I'm not a charity case, Elliot. I can take care of myself."

"I know you can, but if you have someone willing to help take care of you, don't reject that help. You've been in fight or flight mode for God knows how long. Give yourself a break and just let me help you," he says as he takes my hand into his.

"I won't be here long. I promise," I say.

"You don't have a deadline, Maya. You can stay here for as long as you want," he says.

"What I want is to get out of Vegas," I say.

"Technically, we are outside of the city limits right now," he says with a smile. "I mean it. I want you here, Maya. I would be lying if I said that part of this wasn't for selfish reasons, but I want to do this regardless."

"What is selfish?" I ask.

"I want you here because I want to be close to you, Maya. I've never been one to sugarcoat things and I'm not going to start now. You don't deserve to get jerked around so I find that it's going to be far better for you if I am just blunt with you from the beginning," he says.

"Well, start with the blunt part, because that was vague as fuck," I frown.

"Maya, the only reason I work a shift at the bar every week is for you. I don't do that with any other bar that I own. I could be more specific, but I don't think it's the right time for that. Just understand that I want you here. I would not offer if I was not sure," he says.

"I won't get in your way. Just tell me if I annoy you. I'm not fragile," I say. I still don't understand why he would want me here. There's nothing about me that draws anyone in. I'm sure he just feels bad for me because of what happened to his sister.

"I know you're not fragile," he says with a smile. "It's late. You should get some sleep."

"Uh. Yeah. I can just crash on the couch. I don't want to overstay my welcome," I say.

"You are not sleeping on the couch, Maya," Elliot says. "I have a guest room you can take over. I'll get you something to sleep in and we can go get you clothes tomorrow." He takes my hand and stands me up before leading me down the hallway. He goes into the master bedroom, and I wait in the doorway while he grabs a T-shirt.

"Thank you," I say quietly.

"You're welcome," he says with a smile. "If you want to take a shower, you'll have to come use my bathroom. I'm remodeling the main bathroom. I have towels and soap in there. We can get you something a little bit more specific tomorrow."

"Uh... okay," I say. "I feel out of place."

"I know. It'll get easier," he says. "Come take a shower. You'll sleep better." He gestures for me to come into the room. He goes to the bathroom and starts the shower before pulling out towels and a washcloth. I stand there and awkwardly watch him, not knowing what to do.

"Thanks," I whisper.

"You don't have to keep thanking me," he says. "I know it's easier said than done, but try to relax. As much as I know, you don't wanna hear it, you are safe here."

"I know. I'm just not used to feeling out of place like this," I admit.

"Well, give it some time. Soon you will be back to scolding me for not washing glasses right," he says with a smile.

"You really do suck at washing glasses," I say.

"See? Already settling in," he says.

"So making fun of you and your big hands not being able to reach the bottom of the glass is normal?" I ask.

"For you? Very normal," he laughs. "See, if it ever bothers me, I will just put everything up really high so you can't reach it and you are forced to ask for help."

"Oh, that's just rude," I say with a chuckle. It feels weird to laugh, but he makes everything feel better by just being himself.

"I'd advise you not to ignore me then," he says with a grin.

"I'll just buy a step stool with all this money you are going to be paying me," I shrug.

"Already outsmarting me," he laughs. "Take a shower. I'll be here if you need me, okay?"

"Okay," I say. He leaves the bathroom and shuts the door behind him. Instinctively I lock myself in before getting undressed. I need to wash my clothes, so I have something clean to wear tomorrow. I wonder if he would be okay with me washing my clothes.

When I turn and look at myself in the mirror, I focus on my tattoos. They are admittedly beautiful tattoos. They all are a reminder that tomorrow could be different. They also remind me of what they are covering. Although not all of them are covering a scar, a lot of them are hiding something painful that happened to me. My biggest tattoo is on my chest. It is a small bouquet of roses with a snake winding through it. Its highest point is just under my throat, and the lowest portion wraps across my abdomen under my breasts. The flowers on my chest have winding vines that connect to the tattoos on my forearms and are littered with roses and leaves that I later added.

The worst of the scars is on my forearm. John was high out of his mind and cut my arm open from my elbow to my wrist because I made him mad. I have a bad habit of not knowing when to shut my mouth sometimes. I should know better than to backtalk him when he is in a mood like that. For whatever reason, I felt the need to push him further that day. I likely needed stitches, but there was no way he was going to let me go. Once it healed, he paid for me to get it covered up with an array of those vines and roses. It blends in well with the tattoo on my chest that spreads down my arms. In hindsight, I think he did that so no one would ask questions.

I get into the shower and turn it to its hottest setting. I let the scalding hot water wash over me. It's the type of burn that leaves your skin throbbing in its wake. The uncomfortable feeling it gives me is almost euphoric. It serves as a reminder that I am still here and I am still alive. I should not find comfort within the discomfort that I cause myself. I am very well aware of the fact that I am a giant walking red flag for mental health awareness. Sometimes I tell myself that I have the capability of healing myself from all of my hidden trauma, but then I always wrap back around telling myself it doesn't matter because nothing will ever get better. I always find a way to blame myself and think that I deserve the things that have been done to me. Logically speaking, no one deserves the things that I've gone through. Except, maybe, Jonathan.

When my skin is sufficiently seared from the hot water, I get out of the shower. I am not in the habit of showing my ass, so lucky for me, the shirt he gave me almost comes down to my knees. I open the bathroom door and I find that he is changed into pajamas and a plain white T-shirt. He looks different like this, but somehow I find it even more appealing than his usual jeans and T-shirt combo.

Elliot is sitting on his bed looking at his phone. He looks up and smiles when he sees me standing there staring at him. "Is it okay if I wash my clothes?" I ask.

"I can do it," he says as he stands up.

"Uhhh," I say hesitantly. The last thing I need is for him to mention or ask about the blood if he sees it. "I'd prefer if I did it."

"That's fine," he says. "Let me show you where everything is."

I gather my clothing and follow him to the laundry room off of the kitchen. When I toss in my clothes, he puts in soap and starts it.

"I'll be up for a while so I will switch it over for you," he says. "Go get some sleep."

"Okay," I say. "I'd like to try and get a real phone tomorrow if it's not too much trouble."

"Not at all. We can go when you wake up," he says with a smile.

"I'll try to be up at a decent hour. I don't like sleeping late," I say.

"I can come wake you up at noon. Does that work?"

"Yeah. I try to get up at eight, so it'll be nice to sleep some," I say.

"It's four in the morning. I won't even be up at eight," he says. "If you do wake up though, you are welcome to anything in the kitchen."

"Thanks..."

"The guest room is across from my room," he says. I turn to leave and his words stop me.

"And Maya..."

"Yeah?" I ask.

"Don't think I haven't noticed that you never eat," he says. "I won't pester you about much, but I will for that."

"Alright," I sigh. I can't say that I'm surprised. I don't think I've ever eaten around him and I usually work 12 hours on the weekends when I am with him.

I go to the guest room and stare at the bed for a while. Instinctively, I want to lock the door but I know I shouldn't. It's stupid that I even want to go in the first place. I have to force myself to get into bed without locking it.

I stay curled up on my side facing the door. I have this overwhelming feeling that Jonathan will find me and I want to at least be prepared when he comes into the room. If I'm gonna die, I at least like to see it coming. My eyes are getting heavy, but I don't want to look away from the door. Every noise in the house has me on edge. Eventually, my brain unwillingly shuts down and I fall asleep.

Chapter Two

Elliot

Once Maya is in the room, I go to the couch and sit down. I am stuck somewhere between rage and sadness. Everything about this reminds me of Laine. Not a day goes by that I don't wish I had done something different. I have an overwhelming sense of guilt for what happened to her. None of us saw it coming. At the time, we didn't see any of the signs. In hindsight, he was fucking cruel to her.

Maya reminds me a lot of her, but the difference is... Maya is fighting for herself. Laine was either not strong enough to run or was too trapped to try. All things considered, Maya is getting away from Jonathan before he escalates to a deadly level. If he got a hold of her now, it would have deadly consequences. Like fuck if I'm letting that happen to Maya.

She's worked at that bar for four years now. Every Friday night I work a shift with her. I don't necessarily have to work a shift, but I like being around her. Even before I put the pieces together, I loved being in her presence. I've always made sure to be professional and respectful. Obviously, I know what I'm doing to myself by having her stay here. I know it's not going to help the feelings that I have for her, but I can't help but wonder if this could be the start of something. She has a lot of healing to go through, but everyone heals differently.

I'm not going to hide how I feel about her. She deserves honesty, but I'm also not going to push her. If she ever feels the same way about me, it's as simple as letting everything go at her pace.

I pull out my phone and text Daniel to see if he's awake. Knowing him, he's sitting in front of his TV watching some stupid show.

Me: You up?

Daniel: I am. Is everything okay?

Me: Nope. Call me.

Not even ten seconds later, he calls me. "Hey," I answer.

"What's wrong?" Daniel asks. He has been my friend since we were in elementary school. Daniel and Lana have been married for five years. Lana and Maya are a lot alike in the way they carry themselves. They are both self-sufficient and independent women. They have no room for the damsel in distress bit that many women pull. They like being cared for even if they don't want to admit it. They will always choose to take care of themselves before they let anyone else though. This is due primarily to preference, but trauma certainly helps make those decisions.

"Remember Maya?" I ask.

"Fuck. Is she okay?" he asks. He comes into the bar enough to know who she is. He's also the only one I've confided in about my feelings for her.

"Uh. Not really. She's in my guestroom right now," I say with a sigh. "He came into the bar tonight and demanded money from her. She didn't have exactly what he wanted. I heard him slap her, but by the time I got out there to her, he was gone. She told me that she was trying to find a way to get away from him and asked me to hold onto some of her papers. I gave her that phone that I've been holding onto. She hadn't been away from the bar for more than an hour and a half before she called me."

"Shit. What did he do?" he asks. I can hear Lana in the background asking what's going on. "Maya is at Elliot's house."

"She hasn't said much but she said that he hit her again, but then said that she thinks he raped her. I'm not gonna press the issue because she doesn't seem like she wants to talk about it," I say.

"But she's okay?"

"Physically, I think so. I'm not entirely sure. Before she went to lay down, she asked to wash her clothes. There was blood on her shorts. I assume that's why she asked to do it herself so I don't think she knows I saw."

"Probably from whatever he did to her. I would say that if she's hurt badly enough, you will notice eventually. She will not be able to hide the discomfort for very long."

"I don't know. After she got out of the shower, she put on one of my shirts. That woman's legs are covered in scars, so it seems like she can hide her discomfort well. I also don't want to ask her and make her spiral. Simply coming into the house made her panic.," I explain. "She also confirmed my suspicions of never eating. I told her before she went to lie down that I noticed that she didn't eat and that basically, I wasn't going to let her get away with not eating. She just said okay and went into the guest bedroom."

"Have you ever seen her eat?" Lana asks.

"No. Richard generally makes fries or something and she says no when he offers to feed her. She was there for a little over 12 hours today and I never saw her have more than water. It's been nearly sixteen hours and I have yet to see her eat," I say.

"Just keep an eye on her. if she's doing that too often, she could have an eating disorder. But she could also just simply be stressed out. I know that I don't like eating when I'm stressed out," Lana warns.

"Yeah," I sigh. "I want to help her, but I don't know where to start. I'm going to have her help me at the office, instead of going back to the bar. Jonathan would find her there in a heartbeat. I'm making sure to not force anything on her because I know it's not going to help. I'm just giving her options and letting her choose what she wants."

"You need to remember that she is not Laine, Elliot," Daniel says carefully. "If you worry, she will too. Don't give her any reason to think that he's after her unless he actually is."

"My concern is who he gets drugs from. I don't know if she knows he's on drugs, but his name has come up a handful of times with people who owe that Russian family money," I say. "I might be overreacting though."

"Just don't make it a thing unless it actually is a thing. That's all I'm saying," Daniel says.

"Yeah," I sigh. "But hey, it's late as fuck. I'm gonna put her clothes in the dryer and try to get some sleep."

"Keep us updated," Lana says. "Bring her around sometime. The last thing she needs is to continue to feel isolated."

"I'll talk to her and maybe you two can come for lunch on Sunday," I suggest.

"That would be fun," Daniel says. "Then she can watch me kick your ass at cornhole."

"You are overly competitive with that," I laugh. "Goodnight, guys."

We end the call and I go to the laundry room to switch her clothes. Anything that might've been there before is now gone, so I start the dryer. I stopped outside the guest room, contemplating if I should check on her. I don't want to accidentally scare her but I want to make sure she's okay. My worry for her overrides everything and I quietly open the door to check on her. I see that she is curled up in the fetal position facing the door. She is asleep, but she doesn't look like she's resting.

When I get to my room and lie down, sleep does not come easily to me. I can't get Laine out of my mind for long enough to be able to close my eyes without seeing what she looked like when I found her. The fucker shot himself right after he strangled her, but it saved me from killing him myself.

Just as the sun is coming up, I drift to sleep.

Chapter Three

Maya

My eyes fly open and I sit up with a gasp when I hear the door open. "Sorry," Elliot says softly. "I was trying to not startle you.

"Fuck," I sigh. "Sorry." I run my hands down my face. He lays my clothes on the bed.

"Don't apologize," he says. "Get dressed and come eat lunch."

"Uh... okay," I say. He leaves the room, shutting the door behind him.

I don't want to eat, but I have a feeling he won't give up until I do eat. Maybe I can just tell him I'm nauseous and I can get by with it for a little longer. Reluctantly, I get up and get dressed.

When I get to the kitchen, I see that Elliot is plating grilled chicken and asparagus. "Sit," he says, motioning to the table. I don't move and I don't say anything because I don't want to lie to him. I don't want to tell the truth either. I don't want to say that eating anything makes me hate myself even more than I already do. I want to convince myself that I'm not as bad as I think... But his voice in my head reminds me that I am nothing.

"Maya," Elliot says without looking up at me.

"I uh... I'm not hungry right now," I say quietly.

"When was the last time you ate?" he asks as he

takes the plates to the table. I know better than to tell him. The look on his face right now tells me he will just be mad at me. "Maya."

"What?" I snap. When he looks up at me, I panic. He doesn't look mad, but half the time Jonathan doesn't look mad until he's actually hitting me. "Fuck. I'm sorry. I shouldn't have done that." I back away from him even though he's not actually getting closer to me.

"When was the last time you ate, Maya," he asks again.

"I said I'm not hungry. Just drop it," I say forcefully.

"I won't. When did you eat last?" he asks again.

"*Stop it*," I yell at him. "*Stop asking.*"

"Do you know why I'm asking?" he asks calmly.

"*Because you are being nosey? Just drop it. Stop fucking asking,*" I yell. I don't know why I am so angry. Everything he says just enrages me and I can't make it stop.

"Maya... When did you eat last?" he asks softly. I feel like I'm being tricked into a false sense of security and something inside of me breaks when he walks closer to me.

"*God damnit, Elliot. Just stop fucking asking. It doesn't fucking matter,*" I yell.

"It does matter because you and I both know the answer," Elliot says as he takes another step closer to me. His body language is neutral, but I don't trust it. I've been tricked into believing Jonathan too many times to trust it now.

"*It's been three days, okay? Are you happy now?*" I say loudly. "*Just stop it. I said I don't want to eat.*"

"Maya, you need to eat," he says softly.

"*What I need is for you to leave me the fuck alone.*

I'm not your goddamn sister. I don't need saving," I scream. When he takes a few more steps toward me the reality of what I just screamed at him washes over me and I panic. "Please… I'm sorry. I'm sorry. I shouldn't have said that… Please don't"

I turn to run but he wraps his arms around me before I can take a step. "Stop. Please. I'm sorry," I beg as I start to cry.

"Shh. It's okay," he says softly. "You're okay, Maya. I've got you." He has my arms crossed over my chest and he is hugging me tightly from behind, making it impossible to pull away from him.

I fall into hysterics and my sobs are coming out as a scream. Reality is quickly slipping away from me and all I can feel is massive amounts of fear as I spiral. Elliot brings us down to sit against the wall in the kitchen and he keeps a tight hold on me, knowing I will run if he lets go.

Eventually, I stop fighting him and he loosens his grip on me. I turn in his lap and wrap my arms around him and his hold turns into a hug rather than a restraint. When I calm myself down, I sit up and look at him finally. "I'm sorry," I say quietly, sniffing back my remaining tears.

"It's okay," he says with a soft smile as he wipes my tears away. I've not felt comforted like this in so long. Before I can stop myself, I kiss him. I immediately pull away in shock at what I just did. "Oh, fuck. I'm so sorry."

I go to move away from him but he grabs my face and kisses me. His kiss is rough as his tongue darts against my lips and I gasp in surprise. I relax into him and reality blurs as we get lost in this emotionally charged connection.

He abruptly pulls away but presses his forehead to

mine, keeping his hands on my face. "As much as I want this, you aren't ready for this. I can't let you rush yourself into something," he says after a beat.

"I know, but it feels right," I admit quietly.

"I agree," he says as he pulls away to look at me. He searches my face as he brushes his thumb across my cheek. "If this really is something and not just being overwhelmed by emotion, we have plenty of time to get there."

"You're right. I'm sorry," I say quietly.

"Please stop apologizing, Maya. You didn't do anything wrong," he says. "Trust me if it hadn't been you, it would have been me." I smile at the admittance of his weakness for me.

"I'm sorry I screamed at you," I say. "And for mentioning your sister."

"It's okay," he says with a smile. "I knew it was going to happen sooner or later."

"What do you mean?" I ask.

"Well... You were bound to come down from that high of getting away. You were still numb to everything. I knew that eventually, the gravity of the situation would hit you. I didn't think it would be rage, but I knew it would be something," he explains. "For the record... You are nothing like my sister."

"What was she like?" I ask cautiously.

"Some would have called Laine a pushover. For as long as I can remember, she accepted all the shit people put on her and never questioned it. She was the kindest person I've ever known though. She would give everyone the benefit of the doubt and support someone no matter who they were. You could call her at any point in the day and she would drop everything to be there for you," He explains "You are the furthest thing from a pushover. I think you've known for a long time how bad things were, but you just hadn't found a way out. I think you do share her kind nature though. You just know your limits better than she did."

"When did she die?" I ask. "You can tell me to shut up. You don't have to talk about her if you don't want to."

"No, it's fine. Laine died about ten years ago. She was 22," he says as he tucks a stray hair behind my ear. "I was the one who found her when Mom couldn't get her on the phone."

"Oh fuck. That's awful," I gasp.

"Yeah... It fucked me up for a while, but Daniel and my parents helped me a lot. It certainly helped that he also killed himself," he says.

"Daniel... He sounds familiar," I say.

"He should. You serve him every weekend," he chuckles.

"Oh! He's nice. He's one of few who isn't a perv to me," I say.

"That's probably only because his wife would kill him," Elliot laughs. "Lana has requested that I bring you around, by the way."

"Why?" I ask, furrowing my eyebrows.

"Because she says I need to make sure you don't feel isolated. I told them I would talk to you about them coming over for lunch tomorrow," he says. "Let's sit at the table."

We stand up but I don't go near the table. "I'm sorry," I say quietly. "I'm not trying to be difficult."

"All I'm asking is for you to sit, okay?" he says. I nod and follow him to the table. "Are you okay with seeing them tomorrow?"

"It's your house," I say as I sit down.

"That's not what I asked, Maya. I don't want to cause you any unnecessary stress and they don't either," he says.

"Yeah, I'll be okay," I say.

"Can I ask you something?" he asks and I nod. "How often do you not eat for days at a time?"

"Uhhh... Too often," I admit.

"Why?" he asks as he starts to eat his food.

"Just some of the things Jon would say to me got stuck in my head. I got wrapped up in the idea that if I lost weight, he would be happier with me. Maybe he wouldn't cheat. Maybe he wouldn't get so angry... But nothing worked. No matter how much I would diet or exercise, he would keep calling me names and keep telling me I was worthless. If I didn't eat, he didn't hurt me as often," I say. "Or at least that's what I believed to justify not eating."

"Before he said those things, was your weight a concern for you?" he asks.

"No," I admit.

"Why?"

"Because I was healthy," I say.

"Are you healthy right now?" he questions.

"No," I say slowly.

"Why not?"

"Because..." I start to say but stop and frown, making him laugh.

"Go on," he encourages.

"Because I'm not eating. I've been a lot weaker lately," I say.

"Then what do you think your priority should be? Jonathan or your health? I mean, you left for a reason right?"

"Yeah. yeah. I get it," I sigh.

"Aht. No. Say it, Maya," he says.

"Fine. My health should be my priority," I say.

"The first thing you should do is work on differentiating between what he convinced you to be true and what actually is true," he says. "The truth is, I've known you for what... three years? I have never seen you eat. Ever."

"Wait, really?" I ask.

"Mhmm. Richard asks you every time I see you if you want food and you've always said no. You've never brought anything in with you either."

"I don't know how to feel about that," I admit.

"Right, so how many other things do you think there are that I notice, that you don't? How many things are there that he has you blind to?" he asks.

"Fuck... A lot I'm sure," I say.

"Exactly," he says before pointing to my food. "Eat."

"Elliot," I sigh.

"I'm not asking you to eat everything, because if you haven't eaten in three days, you'll make yourself sick if you eat too much," he says. "Just eat *something*. Preferably the chicken, since it has protein."

"You annoy me," I frown.

"I know," he says with a grin before taking a bite of his food.

"Maybe I'm a vegetarian," I say.

"Then eat the asparagus," he shrugs.

"Fine," I sigh and pick up the fork. He diverts his attention to his own food rather than watching me.

"So, I will warn you," he says. "Daniel is going to con you into playing cornhole with him tomorrow."

"I'm pretty good at that game," I say as I take a bite

of my food. The flavors burst in my mouth and it stops me in my tracks. I'm not used to enjoying food.

"He's ridiculously competitive," he says. "Is it okay?"

"Mhmm. Yeah, it's great," I say.

"You don't sound very convincing," he laughs.

"Sorry," I smile. "It just took me by surprise. I'm not used to enjoying eating something."

"Maybe you just suck at cooking and that's why you don't want to eat," he says with a snicker as he eats.

"Rude," I gasp dramatically before laughing with him.

"I could teach you how to cook if that would help," he teases.

"Ya know... Suddenly this food is terrible," I say before taking another bite. "Awful."

"I'm glad you like it," he says, patting my hand. "When we get done, we can go run errands. We'll take the car since you don't have a helmet yet."

"Yet?" I ask with a smile.

"Mhmm. I plan on taking you out more, although last night is the only time you will ever wear shorts," he says.

"Why's that?" I ask.

"Dress for the slide, not the ride, sweetie," he tells me. "If that bike goes down, shorts are the last thing you want to be wearing."

"You're going to make me wear a jacket, aren't you?" I ask.

"Yes Ma'am," he says with a smile. "I like you better with your skin attached."

"If only you knew just how morbid that really was," I say, laughing at my dark joke.

"Mhmm. I have an idea," he says.

"I doubt it, but either way," I say with a smile.

It's only when Elliot stands and grabs my plate that I realize I've eaten everything he gave me. "Go get your shoes," he says simply.

I'm glad he didn't draw attention to me actually eating. I know I need to get past whatever I have going on in my head because he's right, I left for a reason. I can't leave him for hurting me then turn around and hurt myself. I know it's going to be a process and I know I'm going to have moments where I spiral, but I've gotten further than I ever thought I would.

Once I get my shoes on, we go to Elliot's car. The first place we stop is the store to get me a new phone. When we park I give him a weird look.

"What?" he asks.

"I need my money from the bar first," I say.

"A new phone would take all of your money and you'd still have a shitty phone," he says. "I'll just put you on my phone plan and we can separate your line off later if you want."

"Elliot, that's kind of you and all, but..." I start to say.

"But nothing. Come on," he says.

"I'll just pay you back," I shrug before getting out of the car.

Once inside, Elliot tells the sales representative what he wants. Once the phone is paid for and set up, he hands it to me as we are walking out.

"Block his number," he says.

"He doesn't even know the number," I say.

"That's fine. Block it," he says again. I give him a weird look but block Jonathan's number. "Thank you."

"Why did you want me to block him?" I ask.

"Because abusers can be really fucking convincing when they want to gain control back over you, Maya. No matter how strong of a person you are, you are still susceptible to that persuasion. In the kitchen today when you mention Laine... you legitimately thought I was going to hurt you. That fear came from everything he did to you. No matter how safe with me you knew you were, that trigger had already been hit. If he hits that trigger he could make you fold fast and you'll go right back to him armed with a list of excuses on why you think he's better and this time will be different. Blocking his access to you before he can find and hit that trigger makes the difference between healing from his abuse and falling back into that cycle of abuse."

"Thank you," I say quietly. I can't argue with that, because he's right. Jonathan scares the shit out of me and it wouldn't take much to make me fold just for the sake of trying to keep the peace.

"You're welcome, Maya. Let's go get you some clothes and whatever else you need before we go by the bar," he says.

"Elliot, I have money," I say. "I know you do, but I want you to save it. Saving was important to you less than a day ago, so I want you to be able to keep doing that without having to worry about getting what you need to start over," he says.

"I was saving because I was going to move across the country," I say.

"And now? " he asks.

"Now... I don't know what I want..." I say.

"Well... Until you figure it out, I'm still buying you what you need," he says with a smile.

"Fine. It's like arguing with a brick wall anyway," I say and he chuckles.

•••

We spend an unreasonable amount of time buying clothes. I tried to get by with the absolute bare minimum, but Elliot is more stubborn than I am. He made me get everything that I need, which is a lot more than I anticipated. Replacing everything I own has proven to be expensive. If I had a way to get my stuff without getting murdered, I would.

"It feels weird not going to work," I say with a sigh.

"You deserve a break," he says simply.

"Who's working tonight for me?" I ask.

"Fiona," he tells me.

"It's her daughter's birthday. She can't work," I frown.

"She volunteered, Maya. Scold her, not me," he says.

"Why would she do that?"

"Because they care about you," he says as we pull into the parking lot of the bar. "Come on. I don't want you out here alone."

I get out of the car and follow him inside without a word. I have a weird feeling being here and I don't like it.

"Hey. You're driving your car," Richard says. When he sees me he drops what's in his hands and hugs me. "Are you okay?"

"Yeah. I'm okay," I say.

"Why are you assuming she's not okay?" Elliot asks.

"She came in with you and Fiona said you don't work here anymore. That combined with Jonathan calling here fifteen times today looking for you."

"Fuck," I say quietly, backing myself away from

everyone.

"Hey hey hey. You're okay," Elliot says as he pulls me to him to hug me.

"He's looking for me," I whisper.

"I thought I heard you," Fiona says. "Maya!" She grabs me from Elliot and hugs me tightly.

"Hey," I say with a shaky voice.

"What happened? What did he do?" she asks. I give her a strange look and she smiles softly.

"Baby. You are not as good at covering bruises as you think. My ex beat the fuck out of me for months before I left. I knew what was going on but didn't want to force you to say something you weren't ready to say. What happened?"

"He uh... He came in here and got mad that I didn't make what he wanted me to and hit me. When I got home later... he just lost it... I called Elliot and he came and got me," I explain vaguely.

"He didn't know you left?" she asks.

"Uh no... He locked me in one of the rooms so I just went out of the window to get to Elliot," I say.

"I'm glad he was there," she says.

"As far as anyone needs to know, she quit and we haven't seen her since," Elliot says. "Okay?"

"Of course," she says.

"Jonathan is here," Harry says hurriedly as he comes into Elliot's office.

"No no no no," I say as I instantly start crying. I try to back away again but Elliot grabs me and hugs me tightly.

"I've got you, Maya. He can't hurt you anymore. I won't let him," Elliot says softly before kissing my temple.

"I'll handle it," Fiona says. When she turns around

to walk out she stops. "Fuck."

I turn to the door and see that the blinds in the window of Elliot's office are open and I make eye contact with Jonathan. He looks more angry than I have ever seen him. It's the type of rage that gives you an understanding of what someone means when they tell you they were so mad that they saw red. His teeth are clenched so tight that you can see a vein protruding from his temple. His hands are balled into fists and his face is bright red as he holds back all of the murderous desire he has for me right now.

Elliot immediately pulls me behind him and I cover my mouth to keep my sobs quiet.

"*Your fucking boss can't protect you forever, Maya,*" Jonathan screams at me. "*You can't hide from me.*"

Elliot walks away from me and out of the office to close in on Jonathan, and I break down. I walk closer to Elliot in hopes of Jonathan's attention remaining on me and not Elliot.

"Get the fuck out of my bar," Elliot growls.

"Fuck you, man. I'm not going anywhere until Maya comes home with me," Jonathan says.

"She's not going anywhere with you. Get the fuck out of my bar," Elliot says, raising his voice.

"She can speak for herself, or are you making that choice for her?" Jonathan challenges.

Elliot puts his arm around my waist and pulls me closer, wanting me to speak up. "Go ahead," he says to me.

"I'm not coming back," I say quietly. "I should have left a long time ago."

"So you're leaving me for this fucker?" he asks with a familiar venom in his tone. There is no right way to answer this without escalating things.

"I'm not leaving you for anyone. I'm leaving you

because you are abusive and I'm tired of being hurt by you," I say. I am holding onto the tiny shred of confidence for dear life. I can feel the panic bubbling up inside of me and I know I am liable to shut down at any moment. When he chuckles in response, it terrifies me. When he's angry, he comes across as calm and collected. We could be in a crowded room having the time of our lives, and that laugh will instantly strike fear in me.

"Now, get out," Elliot says. Jonathan ignores him and keeps his eyes locked on me.

"What did I tell you would happen if I caught you fucking around with another man?" Jonathan asks.

"It doesn't fucking matter, Jon. Go crawl into bed with one of the many women you cheated on me with and leave me alone. We are done," I say, trying to keep my voice firm.

"We are not done. This needs to be a conversation rather than you blaming me for shit I didn't do," he says. "I know you are struggling, but throwing your shit off on me isn't how you should do this." The fear flips to anger when he tries to make me look like the crazy one. After everything he has done to me, he wants to sit here and say that I'm just struggling and throwing it off on him.

"*We were done the moment I had to climb out of a goddamn window to get away from you. We were done the moment you held me down and raped me,*" I scream at him.

"Rape?" he laughs. "You are kidding me, right? Come on, Maya. You and I both know that is not how that happened." His calm demeanor does something to my head and I can't make the anger simmer down.

"*How many times did you force yourself on me as some sick fucking punishment for when you got mad? Huh? How many times did you hold me down and cut me and tell me*

I'm lucky you don't go deeper?" Everything is coming out so much louder than I intended, but I can't make it stop. I can't pull myself away from this anger.

"Me?" he says. "Honey... Come on... How many times did I try to get you to stop doing that to yourself?"

"*No!*" I shout. I surprise everyone, including myself when I abruptly step forward and shove him. "You don't get to make me look like the crazy one. You don't get to make me out to be the bad guy."

"Maya," he says softly.

"*Stop it,*" I yell again. "*Just fucking stop.*"

"Maya, honey. You took off in the middle of the night. I didn't know what happened or where you went. I have been worried about you and blowing up your phone. Don't you realize how worried I was about you?"

"No, That's not true," I say as I feel myself starting to spiral. He is intentionally doing this. He wants me to break down in front of everyone so that I look crazy. "I'm fucking lucky you don't last long. You really could have hurt me last night."

Instantly his calm demeanor slips and you can see the anger come out. "Stop, Maya," he says simply.

"What? It's true," I say. "You want to talk about how worried you were for me. Were you worried when you made me bleed? Any other man could have put me in the hospital doing what you did to me last night. You yeah... I'm lucky. That's the truth." Pushing back is the only way I can stop myself from spiraling. One of us will break, and I refuse to let it be me.

"Maya," he growls.

"You know... It really does make me stop and wonder how you got all of those women to fuck you," I say.

The moment the words leave my mouth and before he ever even moves, I know he's going to do it. I know Jonathan can only take so much of being belittled before he snaps. Before Elliot can react, Jonathan backhands me across the face. I stumble backward and hit the wall before slumping down to the floor. I can taste the metallic tang of blood. When I touch my lip, I wince in pain from the sting. I pull my hand away and see the blood on my fingertips.

Elliot is on him so fast that Richard and Harry have no time to react either. He swings and his fist connects with Jonathan's face, making him stumble back this time. A pained noise leaves his lips just as Elliot grabs him by the front of his shirt and throws him as if he is weightless. Jonathan crashes into one of the tables closest to the bar.

Suddenly Daniel appears from behind us all and grabs Elliot before he can get to Jonathan. Richard and Harry promptly step into Elliot's path to Jonathan.

"Come on," a woman says, grabbing my hand. She doesn't look very shocked, so I am guessing she is Daniel's wife, Lana.

"Get the fuck out of my bar," Elliot says to Jonathan as he picks himself up. "I promise you, if you come anywhere near her again, I will fucking kill you." Elliot's tone is deep and rumbly. The anger in his words is so clear and it manifests in such a way that it instantly stops Jonathan in his tracks.

"This isn't over, bitch," Jonathan says to me as a warning.

"It is if you want to live to see tomorrow," Daniel says. "I'd advise you to get the fuck out of here before I let him break your goddamn neck." Jonathan hesitates for a moment but turns and leaves the bar.

"Holy fuck, he's got a death wish pulling shit like that," Daniel says, almost laughing. Elliot ignores his friends and comes over to me. I can see it on his face that he wants to hug me, but he's afraid of scaring me after all of that.

"I never said he was smart," I say with a soft smile. He lifts my chin to look at my face. "I'm okay. I saw it coming before he ever even moved."

"You did that intentionally, didn't you?" he asks, cupping the side of my face where I was hit.

"Yeah... He was trying to make me feel crazy and it made me mad," I say, placing my hand over his. He sighs and wraps his arms around me. When I hug him back, he relaxes.

"Damn," Stephen says, throwing back the rest of his beer. "Can I get a refill?"

"Sorry about that, Stephen," Elliot says.

"Nonsense. Beer, bar food, and a show," he says. "The misses will be jealous." I laugh and shake my head at him.

"His tab is on the house tonight," Elliot says to Fiona before kissing my head and leading me back to his office.

"One hell of a way to meet," the woman who helped me up says. "I am Lana."

"It's nice to meet you," I say sweetly.

"Good to see you again, Maya," Daniel says with a smile.

"It's good to see you too," I say.

"I'll try to go easy on you tomorrow when we play cornhole," he says with a grin.

"You and that damn game," Elliot says, chuckling. "We should get back to the house so we can get her stuff put away." He goes to the safe and takes out the papers that I gave him along with an envelope with my name on it.

"Thank you," I say when he hands it all to me.

"We will see you guys tomorrow," Elliot says. "Just text me before you get to the house please."

Chapter Four

Maya

When we get back to the house we bring all of the bags inside and set them in the bedroom I am staying in. I'm overwhelmed looking at the amount of things that were bought today for me. I'm not used to people caring, let alone going out of their way to help me.

"How much was all of this?" I ask.

"Don't worry about it," he says. "We can come put everything away while dinner cooks.

"Okay," I sigh.

"Come help me make dinner," he says. I nod and follow him to the kitchen. I stand against the counter awkwardly while he gathers items from the cabinet and refrigerator .

"What are you making?" I ask.

"We are making pizza," he says. I simply nod and watch him as he washes his hands. "What do you like on your pizza?"

"I haven't had pizza in a while, but generally just pepperoni. I'm not picky though," I say.

I watch as he prepares everything. He has me get various items for him before having me help him assemble them. Once we are done, we put them into the oven and go to put my stuff away.

When I first got here, I felt so out of my element. I

find myself waiting for instructions or asking to leave the room to do something. Every time I do this, he gives me a strange look before telling me that I don't have to ask. These habits of constantly asking for permission to do things are starting to seem like something I learned from Jonathan's abuse. It's instinctive, so I don't realize that I'm doing it until after I've already done it.

I've known Jonathan my whole life. He was always there. When Dad would get too drunk and Mom would send me away so that he wouldn't hurt me, Jonathan provided me comfort. His trailer was two down from mine, so it was easy to be close to him. When Dad died of liver failure when I was nineteen, he was there. I thought that maybe Mom and I could develop a real relationship, but she up and left the day after his funeral. Jonathan was there when she abandoned me.

The first time Jonathan hit me, I blamed myself. I apologized for making him mad and promised I wouldn't push him again. The next time, I was mad at myself for not learning the first time. Every time after, I kept blaming myself. I refused to connect the dots that Jonathan was my Father. The only difference is Dad was a decent person when he wasn't drunk. When he would have periods of not drinking for a few days, no one got hurt. Jonathan hurts me with or without alcohol. No matter if he is high or sober, he will still hit me without remorse.

My entire life has been consumed by Jonathan's abuse, and I am only now seeing that it started far before he ever hurt me physically or even mentally.

I want to break out of this cycle of abuse so badly. I don't want to be like my mother and run straight to another abusive man. Elliot is truly a great man, but I keep finding myself thinking I am not deserving of his affection. How could someone like me catch the attention of a man like him? A man who defends me without a second of hesitation. Someone who values my thoughts and emotions. I don't know how to handle how kind he is to me.

I tell myself that I should just get a bus ticket and run, but what will that accomplish? If Jonathan wants me dead, he will find a way to me. Running seems logical until I remind myself that Mom ran when she didn't even have to. Dad was dead and she could finally have a normal life. She could have had me, but she ran. Staying means rebuilding close to the man who destroyed me piece by piece, and that scares the hell out of me.

I manage to eat dinner without melting down again. I don't eat nearly as much as I did at lunch, but it's a start. I help Elliot clean up before sitting on the couch. As he is scrolling through the movie options, he notices me smile when he passes by a movie. He goes back and chooses 'The Princess Bride' for us to watch.

After a while, he notices that I am getting tired and pulls me down to lay my head in his lap. He simply rests his hand on my side and continues to watch the movie. Being close to him like this brings me an entirely new feeling of peace. My eyes get heavy as he gently rubs my back when I roll slightly on the couch to get more comfortable. Eventually, I close my eyes and don't have the energy to open again.

I

I stir beside Elliot as a thud fills my subconscious. I am wrapped in his warm embrace. Our shared dreams still linger in the air as I peel my eyes open. The bedroom is still and

dark. His soft snores stop when I shake him out of his sleep.
Someone is in the house and the creaking of the
floorboards gives away their location.
They are close.
Panic washes over me as Elliot springs up from
the bed and commands me to hide. I can't leave
him. He should be the one hiding.
He's here for revenge.
He's here for me.
We take quiet steps to the door, but the groan of
the old wooden door reveals us instantly.
Elliot yells at me to run when a face appears in the
hallway painted with a sinister smirk. I grab his
arm and pull him. I want him to run with me.
No...
I need him to run with me.
He will be seen as an obstacle to overcome before
my inevitable death. He will be met with deadly
force as my punishment for disobedience.
A loud bang fills the air and a scream is ripped
from my throat as I watch Elliot slump to the floor.
Blood slowly runs from a hole in his forehead.
I am on my knees begging. I am praying for
him to get up and run away with me.
It's my fault.
His death is my punishment.
A laugh cuts through the utter heartbreak blanketing
my mind and the panic sets back in.
In a flash, he is over me with his hands
wrapped around my throat.
I can't breathe, so I fight.
I grow weaker as the room starts to dim.
His face is painted with the same evil grin when it hits me.

My death is Jonathan's revenge.

I

A blood-curdling scream leaves my lips and I sit up off the couch in a panic. I am sweating profusely and I instantly throw myself into a spiral. Panic and heartbreak flood my brain as I replay the image of Elliot dead on the bedroom floor. I can still hear my pleas for him to wake up bouncing around in my head.

Hands grab my shoulders when I go to get up and run for the door. I let out another ear-piercing scream as I turn and start hitting the figure that has a hold of me.

"Stop, stop, stop. You're okay. It's Elliot," he says as he wraps his arms around me and pulls me to his chest. When I hear his voice I throw my arms around his neck and hug him tightly. When I pull away, I bring my hands to his face, trying to figure out what is real and what is my mind playing tricks.

"Elliot," I whimper. I run my fingers across the spot where Jonathon shot him with tears streaming down my face. "H-He killed you... I saw you die."

"I'm okay, Maya. I'm right here," he says as he pulls me back to his chest.

"It felt so real," I say with a hiccup.

"I know, sweetie. I know it did," he says softly before kissing my temple.

I turn in his lap to straddle him so I can lay my head on his chest. Having his arms wrapped around me as I focus on the rhythm of his heart calms me. When I shift in his lap, I feel the bulge of his growing erection press against my center. He tries to stifle a groan as I gasp softly.

"Did I hurt you?" I say as I try to move away from him, but he holds me in place.

"No, Maya... Never," he says with a silky tone as he shifts and presses himself against me more. A groan slips out of me followed by the rush of realization of what I am feeling right now.

This man is hard... for me. He is holding me firmly in place, almost intentionally ensuring that I feel what I am doing to him. Does he know what it does to me? I haven't felt true arousal in so long that it's overwhelming. I cannot remember the last time I ached to be touched like I am right now. I can hear the quickening of his heart and it's impossible for me to contain my needs.

I roll my hips against his and he groans again. When I look into his eyes, they are filled with desire. I bring my hands to his face and kiss him with another deep roll of my hips against him. He tightens his grip on my waist and I grind against him again.

"You're playing with fire, Maya," he says, his voice thick with lust.

"Here's to hoping I get burned," I say huskily.

"Is this what you want, Maya?" he asks as he pushes his erection against me, forcing a moan from me. He runs his hand up my side to cup my breast and teases my nipple through my shirt.

"Yes," I say without hesitation, pressing against him again.

"Are you sure you want this, Maya?" he asks as he kisses me softly. "We don't have to if you aren't ready." I nod and bite my lip seductively, stifling the urge to beg him.

Elliot brings his lips back to mine. He keeps a hold of me as he stands and I wrap my legs around his waist. I loop my arms around his neck as he carries me down the hall to his room. He maintains his kiss as he lays me down and is settled between my parted legs. When he presses himself against me I break our kiss as I moan.

"You are so beautiful, you know that," he says before kissing down my neck.

"Please," I beg. "Take what you want."

"What I want?" he asks, and I nod. "What I want it to taste you, Maya."

Elliot pulls my shirt off as he kisses down my chest, swirling his tongue around my nipple. My body is tingling with anticipation as he moves down my belly. When he pulls my shorts down, I lift my hips so he can drag them off of me, taking my underwear with them.

When he slowly licks across my clit I moan and arch off the bed as the sensations overwhelm my brain. I haven't felt anything like this before. No one has ever done this before.

Elliot slides two fingers into me as he flicks his tongue across me. "Oh, fuck," I gasp. He starts to slowly work my body as moans freely come out of me.

His pace picks up with every pleasured sound that I make. When I run my fingers through his hair, he pushes another finger into me. He curls them in to hit a spot that makes my eyes roll back as I groan. The feeling of his mouth on me combined with the feeling of him thrusting into my body has my legs shaking.

When he takes my clit into his mouth and sucks, I instantly unravel as an orgasm tears through me. "Oh, Elliot," I moan loudly as I involuntarily rock my hips against him. He sucks harder and I dramatically arch off the bed as my moans get caught in my throat. My body trembles as he pulls my climax out of me. When the feeling fade he moves up to kiss me. The sweet taste of my arousal on his tongue makes me desperate for more.

"Please… Elliot… Please, fuck me," I plead, my body trembling with need. He kisses me once more before moving to get out of his clothes.

When he returns to me, he settles back between my legs. He rubs the head of his cock against my slit.

"Let me know if it hurts," he says as he slowly pushes into me. I grit my teeth and ball my hands into fists as he stretches me to fit him. "Fuck, you feel so good wrapped around my cock," he groans when he bottoms out inside of me.

His movements quicken and I moan softly as pleasure overtakes the discomfort. Each stroke into my body relaxes me as I accommodate to his size.

"Elliot," I whimper.

"God, you take me so well," he says as he slams into me.

"Harder… please…" I cry out.

"Does my girl like it rough?" he asks and I nod. "Come for me, pretty girl. Milk my cock."

Elliot fucks me hard and fast and my moans turn to screams as he easily pulls an orgasm from me.

"That's right baby girl…. Take my seed," he groans as he pushes in and drains himself inside of me.

He moves to lay beside me and pulls me over to lay my head on his chest. We are both breathless and satiated as we lie together on his bed.

"I didn't hurt you, did I?" he asks, breaking the silence.

"God, no," I laugh. He chuckles and kisses my forehead.

I am too exhausted to move, and Elliot doesn't seem to be in a rush to move either. I close my eyes and let the rhythm of his heart lull me to sleep.

Chapter Five

Maya

Elliot's soft voice pulls me from my dreams. "Maya," he says.

"Mmm," I groan and he chuckles.

"Daniel and Lana are going to be here soon," he says. "Come take a shower with me."

"The bed is so comfortable though," I complain as I get up.

"Don't worry, you'll be in it again tonight," he says with a smile as we step into the bathroom.

"I like the sound of that," I smile. He kisses me softly before turning the water on.

When we get in, Elliot takes to washing my hair. I close my eyes and enjoy him taking care of me. I love how attentive he is to me. I could get used to this feeling.

I replay the events of last night over in my head and I remember something he said while we were having sex. "You called me your girl," I say.

"You caught onto that, huh?" he asks as he conditions my hair.

"Yeah," I say with a smile.

"Do you wanna be my girl, Maya?" he asks.

"I do," I admit.

"Good," he says. "I want you in bed with me every night then."

"If we keep doing that, I'm going to need to refill my birth control," I say.

"Why's that?" he asks.

"Unless you want to get me pregnant," I say. He leans into me and places his large hand on my belly.

"I think you'd look lovely carrying my baby, Maya," he says as he kisses and nips my shoulder.

When I moan he moves his hands to my hips. "Elliot," I say softly.

"Do you want that, sweet girl? Do you want me to put my baby in your belly?" he asks as he presses his erection into me.

"Yes," I admit quietly. I want everything that this man has to give me. I want it all.

"Then be my good girl and bend over for me, Maya," he says with a husky tone. I immediately do as he says and bend over, placing my hands on the wall.

With more urgency than last night, he fills me, bottoming out with a growl. His pace grows relentless as he starts to pound into me.

"Oh my God," I moan. "Harder Elliot, please."

"Do you want it? Do you want me to put my baby in you?" he asks as he slams into me again and again.

"Yes. Oh god, Yes," I moan loudly.

"Then beg for it, Maya. Beg for my come."

"Please, Elliot. Please fill me with your come," I beg as my climax starts to peak. "Fuck, Elliot. Breed me. Please."

"That's right, sweetheart, you're such a good girl," he says with a groan. My legs shake as a powerful orgasm moves through me. I moan his name. His pleasure harmonizes with mine as he fills me with his seed.

We are both panting when I turn and he hugs me.

He holds onto me for a bit before cleaning my body and shutting the water off.

"I could do that every day," I say. "My god, Elliot." he chuckles and kisses me.

I wrap up in a towel and freeze when I hear talking coming from the living room. I snap my head to Elliot and he smiles. "I think Daniel and Lana are here."

"I need clothes," I say slowly.

"I'll go grab you something," he chuckles. Elliot gets dressed and leaves the room. When he returns, he hands me some clothes to put on. I put on the shorts and T-shirt after brushing and drying my hair.

When we walk into the living room, Daniel and Lana look over at us and smirk. "Did you have a good shower?" Daniel asks.

"Sure did. Have fun listening?" Elliot asks.

"More than he will admit out loud," Lana laughs.

"At least when Elliot hits it, Maya likes it," Daniel says with a shrug. Lana and Elliot's mouths fall open in shock.

"Daniel!" Lana says with a gasp as she smacks his arm. I burst out laughing and Daniel smiles brightly at the others.

"That was awful, Dan," Elliot says disapprovingly.

"Oh, lighten up," Daniel laughs. "At least Maya likes my dark humor."

"I'm just going to skip past that," Elliot says "We haven't had a chance to go to the store for food just yet, so I'll need to do that."

"Maya and I can do that," Lana says. "Give her a break from all the testosterone in this house."

"Is that okay?" I ask Elliot. He looks sad suddenly. For a split second, I start to panic until he hugs me and kisses my temple. When he pulls away he cups my face.

"You don't have to ask my permission to go somewhere," he says softly.

"I'm sorry. I just..." I stay to say.

"I know. Don't apologize," he says as he kisses me. "Have fun and keep her out of trouble."

"Yeah, good luck with that. I'm going to corrupt your woman, Elliot," Lana laughs. "Get your shoes and we can go." I go into the guest room and put on one of the new pairs of shoes before going back to the living room.

"So just burgers?" Lana asks.

"Yeah, that works," Elliot shrugs. "Take my card."

When he goes to hand me his credit card, Lana glares at him. "I told you that we are paying," she says with a threatening tone.

"Fine. Damn," Elliot laughs and puts his card back into his wallet.

"Be careful, guys," Daniel says as he kisses Lana. "Don't scare Maya, please."

"We'll be okay," she says.

Elliot hugs me and negativity floods my body. I have no desire to leave this house. I know it's just years of abuse that is making me feel this way. "Call me if you need me," he says softly.

I follow Lana outside and we get into the car. I am silent for a while, but she finally breaks the silence. "How are you, really?"

"What do you mean?" I ask.

"A lot going on for you right now," she says. "I am naturally nosey, but I've heard Daniel and Elliot talk about you enough to be invested in your well-being also."

"They talk about me?" I ask.

"In a good way. They knew something was

happening with Jonathan, but they knew that pushing you into talking wasn't how to get you away from him," she says. "How is it staying with Elliot?"

"Honestly... The word I want to use is scary, but it's not a bad thing," I say.

"I can imagine," she says.

"I'm just... I'm not used to being taken care of. I am not used to people prioritizing me in any way," I say. "Elliot is so sweet that it feels like a trap."

"Yeah, I noticed that you asked him for permission," she says. "Is that an impulse?"

"I'm noticing that I do things that aren't normal," I say. "I ask to leave the room and Elliot just tells me that I don't have to ask, but I feel like I do. If I said or did anything that Jonathan didn't like, all hell would break loose. The only thing he didn't do was full on forcing me to have sex. Not until the night I left."

"Full on?" she asks. "He did other things?"

"Uh... Yeah. He'd... Force me on my knees when I made him mad. He did it before work the other day because he shoved me into the mirror and it broke."

"I'm getting the feeling things were a lot worse than what Daniel and Elliot think," she says, glancing at me.

"Yeah. I don't even know where to begin to sort my thoughts. I know he hurt me and I know he brainwashed me with many things, but I don't know how to undo the damage that I've had for my entire life. His abuse is all I've ever known because, before him, it was my Dad beating my Mom."

"I highly recommend therapy. Elliot will be good for helping you day to day with overcoming those habits, but that deep-rooted trauma is better suited for a professional," she says. "I can send you the information for the woman that I see."

"I appreciate that," I say with a smile. "I'm sorry you and Daniel heard all that."

"Don't be," she chuckles. "Daniel and Elliot have known each other for most of their lives. I don't think I can count how many times Elliot has heard or seen Daniel and me."

"Seen?" I ask, raising an eyebrow.

"Yeah," she laughs. "I take it Elliot hasn't gone into much of what he's into?"

"No, but he's fucking intense," I laugh.

"So, they are both pleasure doms. I'd say they are more of a soft dom because their so called punishments are just repeated orgasms. Daniel tries to solve everything with a problem, no matter if that is my anxiety or if I am being a brat," she explains. "They are both exhibitionists, but only around each other."

"So, Daniel has fucked you in front of Elliot?" I ask.

"A few times. Generally he does it to fuck with Elliot. Sometimes it's because I've smarted off one too many times. Daniel won't do it around you, though. Not unless he knows you are okay with it. The same goes for Elliot. They probably won't even bring it up for a long time."

"I mean, I don't care. I just wouldn't know what to do with myself," I laugh.

"Well, I can guarantee that if Daniel ever does that around you two, Elliot will likely do the same. Men are weird, especially those two," she says.

"That's oddly hot," I say and she laughs as we pull into a parking spot at the grocery store. "Why wouldn't Elliot bring that up to me though?"

"He's just protective of you," she says. "Once he is satisfied that you are okay with something, he will release more of that."

"I have a good mind to just text him and tell him I know," I laugh.

"You should. Maybe he will loosen up. He's afraid of triggering you."

"I got triggered just by having to eat. He's going to have to realize that I need him to just be himself." I pull out my phone and text Elliot.

Me: So Lana told me something about you

Elliot: I figured she would lol. What did she say?

Me: She called you and Daniel a softer pleasure Dom.

Me: Also mentioned that you and Daniel are a fan of fucking in front of one another.

Elliot: Texting doesn't convey emotion well, but you don't seem too offended

Me: Not at all. Anything else I should know that you'll be doing to me?

Elliot: That almost sounded like permission, Maya.

Me: Do you trust him?

Elliot: I do

Me: Then, yes. It was permission.

Me: I know you have this thing about pleasing me, but your desires are just as important to me. I want you to take what you need because I now know that you will

keep me as your equal in that regard.

Elliot: Let's talk about this when you get home so I can better judge your emotions.

Me: Okay lol We just got to the store. Be back soon.

I get out as I am typing my message. When I slip my phone into my pocket and look up, I run directly into a man's chest. I gasp and jump backward. "S-sorry. I didn't see you," I say quietly.

The man is dressed in a perfectly tailored suit. He is massively tall and intimidating. He is handsome, but his eyes lack a soul. He has a smirk on his face that sends a chill down my spine. Jonathan scares me, but this man fucking terrifies me. His entire aura is emitting this vibe that tells me he wants nothing more than to break me.

One word. Depraved.

"That's alright, Igrushka," he says in an unmistakable Russian accent. Behind him is another man in an immaculate suite. He looks to be in his mid to late thirties whereas the man I ran into looks old enough to be my father.

"E-excuse me," I stammer as I slip past them and scurry over to Lana. As we walk inside, I glance back and he is in the same spot watching me walk inside.

"That was freaky," she says.

"Did you see the way they were looking at me?" I ask. "Am I projecting?"

"No. I don't like how he was looking at you," she says. "We just need to get what we need and get back."

We hurry through the store and get what we need. I get the feeling that someone is following us so I abruptly stop and turn. All of my fears are confirmed when I see the younger of the two men behind us. He smirks at me and says something in Russian into his phone.

"We need to go. We will order pizza," she says as she grabs my arm and leaves the cart where it's at. We speed-walk out of the store with our heads on a swivel. The man is still following us so the second we get out of the doors, Lana grabs my hand and we run.

When we get to the car, I go to jump in but I am stopped when a hand covers my mouth and pulls me away from the car. I scream against the hand and thrash, trying to escape their hold on me. Lana doesn't get a chance to react or speak when the man who was following us around in the store steps behind her and pushes her against the car. He says something quietly to her and she stills instantly. Her eyes are wide and locked with mine. I have tears streaming down my cheeks.

"Just cooperate," Lana says with a shaky voice.

"Are you going to be good?" the man holding me asks with a thick Russian accent. It's not the man I ran into, so it's a third person. I nod and he uncovers my mouth. "The boss wants to talk to you."

Lana and the man with her walk around to us and I see he has a knife pressed against her ribs. When she gets within arms reach, she grabs me and pulls me to her. The man who grabbed me is likely just a bit older than I am. He opens the door to the SUV behind him and gestures for us to get in.

I hesitate and he narrows his eyes at me. "If I have to make you, it will end up with you two in the landfill," he says cooly.

"Go," Lana encourages. I feel like my legs are going to buckle, but I slide into the SUV. Lana follows me with the man with the knife behind her. The rows are facing each other so I just stare at the man I ran into as it dawns on me that he is a mafia boss. It's the only thing that makes sense. I've served some who talk too much when they drink and like to gloat about their involvement. Is that why he wants to talk to me?

"Thank you for meeting with me, Maya," he says with a smile.

"I don't feel like you gave me much of a choice, but you're welcome," I say bitterly.

"Do you know why you are meeting with me?" he asks. I don't say anything for a second while I think.

Jonathan is the only person that I know who would be even remotely involved with the mafia. I know he gambled a lot and does cocaine. Maybe he pissed them off so they are coming after me? Maybe if they know I left him, they'll go away.

"Jonathan," I say after a beat.

"Beautiful and smart," he says as he drags his eyes across my body. "Do you know who I am?"

"I do not," I reply honestly.

"My name is Nikolai Petrov," he says. "Jonathan owes me a sizable amount of money."

"With all due respect, I don't give a shit what he owes you," I say bluntly. "He abused me for years and I only just now was able to get away from him. He is no longer my concern."

"But see, Maya, when he made a deal with me to clear his debt in exchange for you, it became your problem," he says as he leans forward to rest his elbows on his knees.

"What is that supposed to mean?" I ask frowning.

"It means, I will get what I am owed," he says with a sinister smile. "Now, you can either pay me what he owes, or I will collect on my deal with Jonathan."

I stare at him in shock. Lana is squeezing my hand so hard that my fingers are going numb. "How much does he owe you?" I sigh heavily.

"Five hundred thousand dollars," he says simply.

"What?" I snap. "I have two hundred dollars to my name. How the fuck am I going to come up with that?" I ask.

"That's not my problem, but you have two months," he says.

"Fine," I say. I just want to get out of this vehicle and get back to Elliot.

"If you try to run, I will kill everyone you know and love. And I will start with Lana." he moves his eyes to Lana before looking back at me. "But I might have to have a little fun with her first."

"Okay," I say curtly.

"I always collect, Ms. Sparks," he continues.

"I said okay," I say through gritted teeth. "Can we go?"

"You may go," he says. The man next to Lana knocks on the window and the door comes open. The man and Lana get out but Nikolai grabs my arm and pulls me to him where I am nearly sitting in his lap. "You have two months to pay or I will collect you myself."

"I understand," I whisper.

"Make no mistake, Maya. When I add you to my collection, you will be used how I see fit. My Igrushka to break," he says quietly. "You understand, don't you?"

"Yes," I choke out. He releases his grip on me and I hurry out of the SUV. The man releases Lana and she shoves me into the car before running around to get into the driver's seat.

I lay my head back to decide if I'm going to throw myself off a bridge or not. Somehow, even in death, I don't think I can escape this. He will just go after everyone I care about. Lana puts her phone to her ear as she tears out of the parking lot.

"Meet us outside when we get back... No, Daniel. We're not okay," she snaps. "No... The fucking mafia just cornered us... Jonathan fucking traded her to them or something... She's not talking... His name is Nikolai Petrov. He said that Maya has to pay five hundred thousand dollars or he will take her... No like fucking kidnap her, Daniel... I don't think we are being followed, but they are going to watch her. I'm sure of it... We will be there in a second... Love you." Lana ends the call and takes my hand.

"I'm fucked," I say quietly. "I can't come up with that kind of money in two months."

"He gave you two months? How the fuck does he expect you to find that kind of money?"

"He doesn't," I sigh. "He said when he adds me to his collection, he will use me how he sees fit."

"What the fuck does that mean?" she asks, knowing what it means.

"It means he's going to rape me or have someone else do it," I say. "He will get what he is owed."

"*Fuck!*" she yells. "I'm going to fucking kill Jonathan."

I stare out of the window as we drive. I am numb to everything, but I know it will sink in. When we pull into the driveway, Elliot and Daniel are in the driveway waiting. Lana doesn't even get the parking brake set before Elliot slings the door open and pulls me out.

I let him hug me tightly but I am plagued with

guilt. I just dragged all of them into this because I went to Elliot for help. Now they are going to feel obligated to help me, even though it could get them killed.

Elliot leads me inside and sits me on the couch before sitting on the coffee table in front of them. "I need you to talk to me, Maya," Elliot says. Daniel and Lana are sitting on either side of me, knowing I am seconds from picking an emotion and blowing up.

"What do you want me to say?" I ask flatly.

"What are you thinking?" he asks.

"That you three should keep your distance from the sinking ship," I say as I stand. Elliot grabs my hand but I yank it away from him and turn to walk away from him. Daniel immediately stands and blocks me.

"Maya," he says cautiously.

"Move," I say.

"No, Maya," he says softly.

"Move, Daniel," I demand, raising my voice. Lana is behind me and Elliot is standing to my side. When he doesn't move I scream it. "*Move!*"

"Sit and talk with us," he says calmly.

"*About what*?" I scream at him. "About how if I run your wife is going to get raped and murdered, because of me? About how when I can't pay he's going to take me? About how if I just killed myself instead, you all would still die? What do you want to talk about Daniel? What is there to talk about? I have to choose between getting kidnapped and raped until he's done with me or get all of you killed. Why the fuck do any of you want anything to do with me? Because if you have an idea, I am all fucking ears."

"I have some savings and so does Elliot. Elliot's parents are on their way over to…"

"No," I laugh. "Absolutely not."

"Maya," Elliot says softly.

"*What?*" I yell as I snap my head to look at him before turning to face him. "You are not giving up everything you worked for for me. It's not happening."

"Maya, we want to do this," he says.

"*No*," I scream. "No. No one wants to do this. You think you want to because you feel obligated to. You decided to help me get away from Jonathan and now you think this is a part of it."

"Maya, honey," He goes to say but I cut him off.

"*No*," I yell again, tears sliding down my cheeks. "Just let me go. I'm not endangering you guys. I'm not taking what's not mine to take."

"Go?" he asks. "Go where?"

"To Nikolai. I can't come up with that money, Elliot. I can't," I say as the front door comes open and a middle-aged couple comes inside.

"Maya, do you hear yourself right now?" he asks softly.

"*Yes, Elliot,*" I scream at him as I start crying. "You're not paying it. I won't let you do that for me. I won't. Just let me go and go on about your life."

"Damnit, Maya," he snaps at me and I flinch. "I love you, Maya. I have watched you from a distance for three goddamn years. I have seen cuts and bruises on you that you made excuse after excuse over. I fell in love with you just dreaming of the future I plan to give you."

"You don't mean that," I whimper, shaking my head.

"Yes, Maya. I mean every fucking word," he says. "I will not let you sit here and sacrifice yourself because you are too afraid to let me love you. I don't care if you get mad at me or not. Hate me, if it makes you feel better. I will not sit here and let you give yourself over to him."

I want to believe him, but I need to get away. I need to be alone. They won't leave me alone. I turn abruptly and slip past Lana before she or Elliot can grab me.

I run to the master bedroom and lock the door behind me before locking myself in the bathroom.

I can't think straight. I just need the noise in my head to stop. I press my palms to my forehead and pace the length of the bathroom while I try to calm myself down. I hear banging on the bedroom door as the others try to get to me.

I remember that the bathroom window isn't far off the ground so I go to it and try to open it.

Fuck, It's jammed.

I need to find something to pry it open. I have to get away. I won't let them get hurt for me. No one can come up with that kind of money. I won't let him pay this debt. I don't deserve his love. I don't deserve anything good he has to offer.

I go to the drawers and start searching for something to help me get the window open when I see it. It's sitting in the corner of the drawer, begging me to take it. I hear them get through the bedroom door and set in on the last obstacle before they stop me from running.

Seeing that stainless steel straight razor sitting there, begging me to pick it up, I make my choice. I'll choose death over watching everyone I love die. I'll choose it over running. I'll choose it over becoming his collectible. I choose to end my life before Nikolai has a chance to do it for me. I won't survive being his captive, so I choose how I leave this world.

I grab the razor and flip it open. Its edge is perfect

for what I need it for. I know what to do to ensure that no one can help me. I only fear failing. I know that slipping away will only bring me peace.

I press the razor to my wrist, preparing to let it dig in and tear through my flesh. A rush of excitement floods me as it starts to dig in and a flood of crimson escapes my skin in the wake of the blade. Everything is still... calm. I am calm when I make myself bleed. I am in control when I have control over my life. No one gets to choose death for me, even if my choice does lead to more carnage. At least I get to leave this world knowing they are safe and alive.

The bathroom door slams against the wall just as Elliot rushes me. When he grabs my arm and pulls the razor away from me, reality slams down on me.

"*Stop,*" I scream. "*Stop it. Let me go.*"

I can't hear anything that anyone is saying over the rush of blood in my head. I scream again and try to pull away when he puts a towel over my fresh cut and wraps his hand around my wrist to apply pressure. The weight of what I've done brings me to my knees. My voice breaks as I continue to scream. All of the pain throughout my life is flooding out of me and it's blinding. The knowledge that I will be used until my inevitable death for something beyond my control is crushing.

Elliot keeps a firm grip on my wrists while he has my arms crossed over my chest. I start to feel dizzy when my breath catches in my throat and I can't get any oxygen. Panic takes over when I can't breathe.

"You need to breathe, baby," I hear Elliot say in my ear. He sounds so distant as everything starts to tunnel. He moves us into the shower before bringing us down to the ground. I am sitting between his legs, lying against his chest where he has me pinned.

"Turn it on cold," I faintly hear Elliot command someone. When the ice-cold water sprays out and hits me, I gasp dramatically. I relax when oxygen rushes through my brain, but the tears continue. I am drenched now and Elliot keeps a firm grip on me. "Breathe, baby. Just breathe. I've got you."

"I'm sorry," I sob.

"It's okay, Maya. I promise it's okay," he says before kissing my temple.

"I shouldn't have done that," I say with a broken voice.

"I love you, Maya. I'm going to help, and you are going to let me," he says firmly. "We are going to figure this out because you deserve the life I want to give you. If they take you, I will find you. If they hurt you, I will heal you. You will survive this, Maya. I won't let you give up."

"I think I'm falling in love with you and I can't make it stop," I cry. "I'm scared it's all going to disappear and it'll be my fault."

"I'm not going anywhere, Maya, and neither are you. No matter where you are, I will find a way to get you back to me. Okay?"

"Okay," I sniff.

"I need to look at your wrist. Is that okay?" he asks and I nod.

Elliot loosens his grip on me before moving the towel to look at my arm. I cut deep, but not so deep that it will need stitches. He got to me in just enough time before I did any major damage.

Daniel appears in front of me and helps me up. "I'm sorry," I say to him.

"Don't worry about it," he smiles softly. "Let's get you bandaged up and we can order some food, huh?"

"Yeah," I say quietly.

Lana brings clothes into the bathroom and then stands with Daniel by the door. I don't even have to ask to know why they are staying while Elliot helps me change clothes.

They are afraid that I'll do something again. I won't, but I understand why they think I will. I don't think I've ever sunk that deep into mania before. At the peak of that episode, I wanted to die. Looking back on the situation, I don't. I want to fight.

So what... he's going to kidnap me. He will have his fun and I will plot my escape. I escaped Jonathan, I can escape them. They don't realize they are taking somebody who was born and raised to withstand abuse. There is nothing they can do to me that will ever top Jonathan or my father. Nothing.

I will survive this because survival is all I know. I didn't fight for twenty-five years to just give up because some jackass wants to forcibly fuck me to clear a debt. Knowing that it's going to happen will only help me prepare my mind. I know it will be different when it actually happens, but again, I survived Jonathan. I will survive Nikolai Petrov.

When I am changed into dry clothes, Daniel takes me to the bed to sit so he can bandage my arm while Elliot changes.

"I feel like an idiot," I admit.

"Why? Because you're scared and you have emotions? How dumb," he says with a smile.

"Touché," I say with a weak smile.

"You have spent your entire life not knowing what love feels like. I know it's probably confusing as fuck to be in a relationship with someone who's nice. Not having to walk on eggshells but still feeling like you should is likely mentally draining. Add that up with the mafia coming after you, anyone would melt over that. Everyone reacts to trauma differently, your anger happens to be directed at yourself," Daniel says as he finishes badging my arm.

"Nikolai is going to get to me. Even with you guys helping with the money, he's not interested in it at all," I say.

"I know," Daniel says. "But you know what?"

"I'll survive," I say.

"Yes ma'am," he says. "We will do what we can to get the money together, but we all need to face the reality that he may very well come for you sooner. He's a mafia boss... they aren't known for being trustworthy." I smile because it's refreshing that he's not bullshitting me.

"Daniel," Lana scolds him.

"It's okay," I say.

"It's not," she says.

"Why? Would you rather me blow smoke up her ass and tell her she's safe? She's not safe, Lana. Jonathan sold her out to the fucking mafia," she snaps at her.

"I know," she says softly.

"Lying to her is going to make damn sure that it breaks her when they do get ahold of her," Daniel continues.

"Despite all of that, I'm not fragile," I say. "I have spent my entire life being subservient to others. I can keep up that façade for the sake of surviving. I'm not saying it won't fuck me up, but it won't be anything like what you just saw."

"What happened?" Daniel asks when Elliot sits beside me.

"Uh... it just all hit me at once that I have never

had a healthy relationship with anyone, friends, family, or a partner. It's always been toxic. So having you guys around fucks with my head. It's like I'm just waiting for the other shoe to drop and I find that one thing that gets me hurt, but that never comes. I tend to self-sabotage before anyone gets the chance to hurt me. Even with Jonathan, if I saw that his mood was turning bad, I would intentionally say something to push him over the edge, because the anticipation leading up to that was worse than what he actually did," I explain. "I don't self-harm often, mostly because Jonathan was always there to do it for me. I did not need to do it when I was always cut up anyway. When all of those feelings suddenly went away, I think it just shocked my system or something."

"I want you to be honest with me when I ask this," Elliot says and I nod. "Are you okay? I don't think being locked in a hospital while the mafia is after you is a good idea, but I also don't want to wake up to find that you've killed yourself."

"I'm okay," I say.

"Do you understand why I am struggling to fully believe that?" he asks.

"When you just had to pry a straight razor out of my hand?" I ask. "Yeah. I understand. I also know that I can say it a million times that I'm okay but you are still going to worry about me. If it wasn't that, you would be worrying about something else."

"If you ever get like that again..." he says but stops before saying it.

"Is this the part where you threaten to punish me?" I ask with a smile. I need him to lighten up a bit. When Daniel laughs, Elliot smiles.

"I'd act on that challenge if my parents weren't

here," he says before kissing me.

"Oh… right," I say. "I don't think I want to go out there now."

"Why?" Elliot asks, confused.

"I just acted like a psycho," I say. "Hard pass. I'll just hide in here and read."

"Trust me. They're not judging you," Elliot says. "They likely won't even bring it up. Mom is a nurse practitioner so she might wanna look at your arm later, but she won't ask you any questions."

"I don't know," I hesitate.

"Trust me?" he asks and I nod. He takes my hand and stands me up before walking me out of the room.

The couple is sitting on the couch and both smile brightly, when they see us. "Hey," the woman says as they both stand.

"Hey Mom," Elliot says as he hugs her, then the man. "This is Maya."

"It's nice to meet you, Maya," the woman says sweetly. "I am Brandy and this is Arthur."

"Hi Maya," Arthur says. Normally father figures freak me out but he doesn't. He seems kind.

"Alright. Let's sit and order pizza and I'll tell you what's going on," Elliot says as he pulls me in his lap when he sits on the ottoman.

Chapter Six

Maya

Elliot explains everything to his parents from him helping me escape Jonathan, to the things he did to me, to the mafia. They listen and nod as he talks. When the pizza arrives we all eat while they discuss how to come up with a half million dollars.

"Well..." Arthur says. "In my experience, they would not let someone rack up that much debt before they tried to collect. I am guessing that they are intentionally giving an outrageous number in hopes of you not being able to come up with it."

"Why not just take her then? Also, why do all of this because she's connected to someone that owes the money?" Daniel asks.

"I don't think it really has anything to do with Jonathan," Brandy says. "Is there any chance you've had interaction with them before?"

"I mean, I'm pretty sure I've served a few of their members at the bar. They talk a lot. They've done that with Fiona also though. They've never said anything important."

"No... They'd only go this far if they wanted to prove a point. They are intentionally trying to scare you, so I honestly don't think it matters if you pay or not," she says.

"But why?" I ask.

"Elliot said your dad died, right?" she asks.

"Yeah. When I was nineteen. My mom moved away shortly after," I say.

"Were you there?" she asks.

"I found him. The medical examiner told us that he had liver failure.," I say.

"What's his name?" Arthur asks.

"Armen Sparks," I say.

"Armen" Lana asks, raising an eyebrow.

"Yeah," I say. "Well, I guess *technically* that's not his last name. He took Mom's last name when they got married."

"What was it before?" Lana asks.

"Oh fuck," I gasp and cover my mouth.

"What?" Elliot questions as he rubs my back.

"His original last name was Volkov," I say slowly.

"So your dad is Russian," Brandy asks.

"I don't know. They literally never talked about their families. The only reason I know his original last name was Volkov is because after he died, I found their marriage license," I explain. My heart feels like it's going to jump out of my chest. It's his fault. Dad did this to me. How did Jonathan get involved though?

"So we need to find out who he was before your mom," Elliot says.

"He didn't have an accent though," I say.

"That just means he didn't grow up around anyone with an accent," Brandy says.

"I'm pretty sure he grew up in an orphanage. When I was like five or six he told me I should be lucky that I have parents to take care of me because he didn't have that luxury," I say.

"Did he have a record?" Daniel asks me.

"I have no idea. I'm sure I could easily go up to the police department and ask but that sounds like a really stupid idea," I say.

"Yeah. Let's not go there. That will make things worse," Elliot says. I sigh heavily and lay my head on Elliot's shoulder.

"I don't like feeling like I'm not in control," I say. "I don't see any way out of this."

"Remember what I said?" he says.

"Yeah," I whisper.

"No matter what happens, I *will* bring you back to me. I will find you and I will fix whatever they've done. You are too strong to let them break you," he says.

"I'm going to kill Jonathan," I say after a moment.

"Yeah. He's a dead man walking," Daniel says.

"I think we need to find him and talk to him," Lana says. "If she pisses him off, there is a good chance that he will slip up."

"I wonder if he knew that my dad was Russian," I say.

"Call him," Elliot says. He picks my phone up off of the coffee table and hands it to me.

I navigate to unblock his number before calling. I put the phone on speaker so that everyone can hear.

"Hello," Jonathan answers.

"It's Maya," I say simply.

"Ready to come home yet?" he asks.

"No. I told you I'm not coming back," I say. "Care to explain why I was cornered by the mafia today?"

"Damn, today? They were fast about that," he laughs. "I'll make you a deal, Maya."

"God. What?" I sigh.

"Come home and I'll make it go away," he says.

"Yeah, I think I'd rather be raped by Nikolai, than go back to you," I say flatly.

"How much did he say that you had to pay?"

"Five hundred thousand dollars," I say. "He said it was your debt and he made a deal with you. Honestly, none of it really makes sense. It's become obvious that there's a piece of this puzzle that I'm missing."

"A massive one," he laughs.

"Is this about my Dad? I know that he was Russian."

"Ahh, see that, you'll have to meet with me to find out," he says.

"Just tell me, Jonathan. After everything, I feel like you owe me at least this."

"I owe you nothing, Maya," he says with a chuckle.

"God, you're worse than my father, you know that? You are a sorry piece of shit. At least he was a good person when he wasn't drinking," I say.

"Don't compare me to that asshole," he snaps.

"I will. He beat the shit out of my mother for no fucking reason, but he never touched me. He rarely even raised his voice with me. You... you hurt me in every possible way. You constantly were looking for something to get mad at me over. He had demons that he treated with alcohol. You are just a demon. There is no redemption for you," I say calmly.

"*At least, I didn't run away from my problems. Like father, like daughter,*" he yells.

"What is that supposed to mean? Do you think it's a bad thing that I decided to put my life ahead of your abuse?"

"Armen was a weak man. He was born weak, he ran away weak, and he died weak. You are no different. You will die just as weak as he did by Nikolai's hand and I made damn sure of that."

"So Dad knew Nikolai?" I ask.

"Jesus Christ, Maya. Yes," he sighs. "Armen worked for Nikolai before you were born. He was his right-hand man. Your mom got pregnant with you and they ran away. He made the mistake of stealing money before he went."

"And you told him who my father was?" I ask.

"Yes."

"What the fuck is wrong with you? Did you ever give a fuck about me? Or are you just bitter because I left?" I say, raising my voice. "You do realize what the fuck this man wants to do to me, right? You realize you just signed my death warrant because you forced me to leave."

"*I didn't force you to do anything,*" he yells.

"You raped me and locked me in the room, Jon. Earlier that day, you shoved me into that mirror and hurt me. Then you blamed me and forced yourself on me too. The vast majority of my scars are because you held me down and hurt me. Do you want to say that you didn't force me? Every time you hurt me you were forcing me out of the window. I shouldn't have had to climb out of a window to get away from you. That shouldn't have been my only option."

"And now you're fucking your boss. What an upgrade," he laughs.

"I don't know why that matters," I say. "My relationship with Elliot is none of your fucking concern, but for the record, he is twice the man will ever be. He doesn't have to beat me into submission. Can we get back on topic, or do you wanna continue this pissing contest with someone you already lost to?"

"God, you are such a bitch you know that?" he asks.

"You made me this way, Jon. This is *your* fault."

"You are a grown-ass woman. Don't blame me for your decisions."

"Isn't that fucking convenient of you to say now. How many times did you blame me for you beating the shit out of me? How many times did you tell me it was my fault because you held me down and cut me open before assaulting me?" When he doesn't say anything I laugh. "Does it not go both ways?"

"Unless you come home, I hope you learn to enjoy what he will do to you because you damn sure won't survive it," Jonathan says simply.

"That's where you are wrong, Jonathan. I *will* survive Nikolai but you won't survive me. I am vowing to you right now that if Nikolai Petrov touches me, I will kill you myself," I say.

"Yeah. Okay, Maya. Whatever keeps your spirits up before he locks you in his basement," Jonathan laughs. "I'll be sure to visit you though."

I end the call and block his number back before tossing my phone to the coffee table. "So what now?" I ask.

"We try to come up with the money and hope that they'll take it and not you," Elliot says.

"I wonder how quickly I would die if I just went to the police," I sigh.

"The logical thing to do would be to go to the police, but in this case, I'm sure it doesn't matter," Elliot says.

"Tomorrow I'm going to try to reach my Mom and see if she can give me anything," I say. "At least something to tell me what I'm getting myself into."

"Do you think she will answer?" Lana asks.

"Yeah, she will. She'll just try to get off the phone as soon as possible," I say. "I'm guessing she ran when Dad died because of the mafia. It sounds like they killed him."

"Yeah. If they found him they would've killed him," Arthur says.

"I feel a little bitter that Mom didn't even warn me," I say.

"Well, give her a chance to explain. She might've just thought you were safe and better off without her near," Lana says.

"I would have been if not for Jonathan," I say, rolling my eyes.

"So, between all of us, I don't think it will be an issue getting that money together," Arthur says. "It'll take a few weeks for us, but it won't be an issue."

"We need to find out how to get them the money," Brandy says.

"They're outside," Elliot says. "A blacked-out SUV stopped at the end of the driveway when you two pulled in."

I abruptly stand and go to the window. Everyone else jumps up with me to see what I'm doing. "Chill out. I'm just seeing if they're still there," I say.

When I look out of the window, the same SUV that we were in earlier, is sitting out at the end of the driveway. I doubt Nikolai is the one sitting out there so I bet it's one of the other guys.

"I'll just go ask, since they want to just sit there and watch me," I say as I go to the door. Elliot promptly puts his hand on the door to prevent me from opening it. "Maya," he says softly.

"I'm not an idiot, Elliot, and neither are you. He said two months, which realistically gives me about a month before I have to actually worry about being taken. His answer on how to get the money to him will tell me if he's actually going to let me pay."

"Okay," he says. "But Daniel and I are coming with you."

"I figured," I say. He moves his hand and I open the front door. Elliot and Daniel follow behind me as I walked to the end of the driveway. When I get to the SUV, the window comes down.

"Hello, Maya," the man greets.

"What is your name?" I ask.

"Why?"

"Because if you are going to stalk me, I would like to know your name," I say and he chuckles.

"Alexi," he says.

"Well, Alexi, I need to talk to Nikolai," I say.

"That's not how this works, Maya. He's not going to come just because you called," Alexi says.

"Then I could just call the cops and tell them I know who killed my dad," I deadpan.

"I'm going to have fun with you, Ms. Maya," he says with a smirk as he puts his phone to his ear. He talks to someone in Russian while we have a staring contest. When I hear my father's name, I smile. It's good to know that my father is his weakness. Now I just need to figure out if it's going to lead to my death or his obsession with me.

"You two okay?" I ask Elliot and Daniel. They are both seething at Alexi's threat to me. Somehow, it doesn't bother me. The only thing it's doing is fueling my desire to kill Jonathan. Nikolai and Alexi will do fine for now.

I'm tired of being the victim. Anyone who puts their hands on me will get added to that list with

Jonathan. I don't care if I go to my grave trying to rid the world of them, I will still try.

"Yeah," Elliot says softly. Alexi ends the call and opens the door to get out, prompting Elliot to pull me back a few steps.

"Relax, Elliot," Alexi says with a chuckle. Elliot stays quiet but glares at him as he and Daniel pull me away to talk to me.

"Why do you want to talk to him other than what you came out here for," Elliot asks.

"I want to ask about my dad. I just don't want to ask while I'm being held hostage by him," I say quietly. "I doubt he will give me any answers, but I can tell that Dad is his and Alexi's weakness."

"I'll agree with you there. If Jonathan is right that your Dad stole from him, I am guessing he's not wanting to kill you. You'd be dead already if that was the goal," Daniel says.

"So he's just going to make me his play-thing until he gets sick of me or whatever debt Dad had, is resolved," I say.

"That's..." Elliot starts to say.

"Depraved? Sick? Yeah, I know. Fortunately for me, I got used to that type of thing with Jonathan. Nikolai is more intimidating and terrifies me, but I know what Jonathan is capable of. They are both sick fucks but that's the story of my life, so I'll be fine."

I glance over and see that another vehicle has pulled up, but this time pulls all of the way into the driveway. Alexi starts walking toward us and motions for us to go back toward the house.

"Let's go inside, hmm?" Alexi says with a smile.

"He's the one who had a knife on Lana," I tell Daniel.

"Good to know," Daniel says, glaring at Alexi.

We walk past the SUV that has Nikolai in it and go up to the porch where Lana, Arthur, and Brandy are standing. "They are coming in. Don't get us killed," Elliot says to his Dad before pointing for them to go inside.

Elliot and I wait for Alexi and Nikolai to step past us into the house before we walk in and shut the door.

"Have a seat," Elliot says to them as he pulls me to sit in his lap on the ottoman so Daniel can sit with us.

"You two are protective of her, no?" Nikolai asks.

"Yes," Elliot answers and Alexi chuckles.

"What happened to your arm?" he asks, pointing to my wrist.

"Shaving accident," I say with a deadpan expression, making Daniel look at me and chuckle. "You knew my dad," I say.

"I did know your Dad. How is he?" Nikolai asks.

"Dead, but you knew that. You should know that you can't trust Jonathan with information," I say. "He has a loud mouth when he's pissed and I know every button to push."

"I'll keep that in mind," Nikolai says with a conniving smile. "He tells me that you left him for your boss?"

"You mean I escaped out of a window because he would beat and assault me almost daily and Elliot helped me get away? Yes, I did. I didn't ask you to come here to talk about him."

"You remind me of your father," Alexi says. "Stubborn and kind."

"Is that why you two killed him? Because he was stubborn?" I ask. "For the record, I don't care that you killed him. Because you think you can somehow use him dead, or even my Mother, as some kind of leverage or something over me... Understand that the world is a better place without him in it. Whatever demons tormented him are gone, so, therefore, one of my many demon's is gone as well."

Alexi curls his face up in confusion when I speak negatively of my parents. It's almost as if he is offended. I laugh and shake my head.

"What's funny?" Nikolai asks.

"You think my Dad was a good person, don't you? Even despite stealing from you," I ask.

"He was too good for the work he did for me," Nikolai says. "His only mistake was stealing rather than simply asking."

"Tell that to my Mom who I watched get beaten daily for as long as I can remember," I say. "He might have been a good person, but alcohol ruined him and my mother."

"Where is she now?" Alexi asks.

"Why? Wanting to threaten to rape her next?" I ask and he smiles. God, he pisses me off more and more every time he smiles at me like that. It's as if he's thinking of all the ways he wants to degrade me.

"What else did Jonathan tell you about your Father?" Nikolai asks.

"That's it. He said Dad worked for you before I was born and he stole from you when he ran," I say vaguely.

Nikolai leans forward to rest his elbows on his knees. He has a pleasant look on his face, but I sense he knows I am holding back.

"What else?" he asks.

"Do you want a play-by-play?" I ask. "He said specifically that Dad was your right-hand man. I assume that is Alexi now though."

"He ran when your mother got pregnant with you," Nikolai says.

"Okay," I say. "I am failing to understand how that's my problem. Clearly, you lied and this has dick to do with Jonathan. I'm sure Jonathan just told you who my father was because I pissed him off."

"How did you piss him off?" Alexi asks and Lana laughs.

"He was just being manipulative," I say. "I said something that pissed him off and he hit me in front of Elliot," I say.

"I take it that didn't go well for him?" Nikolai asks.

"His face is busted up, so I assume not," Alexi says.

"Elliot punched him then threw him across the bar," Lana says.

"Anyway," I say. "You want five hundred thousand in two months, yes?"

"Mhmm," Nikolai says with a smirk. "Plus interest."

"Jesus fucking Christ," I sigh. "Just tell me what you want from me."

"If you wait the entire two months, it's double," he says simply.

"And If I don't pay?" I ask.

"Then you have to come stay with me for a while," he says. "The debt will be paid."

"Is that what my Dad stole?" I ask.

"It is," he says. "With some added interest."

"Why not just go after my Mom? Why me? I hardly existed at that point."

"Who would want to fuck a used-up whore? Maya," Nikolai says bluntly. "It's very simple. You pay every dime of what I am owed, or I own you until it's paid. You'll do as I say during that time, or be punished and have time added."

"You are insane," I say. "I hope you know that."

"That may be true, but it doesn't change the fact that I have the power here," he says. "To note, the others will be watched during this time and if they think about coming near you, even if it's to rescue you, they're just as dead as you'll be. I do not want to kill you, so I'd advise they heed my warning now."

"How long?" I ask. "If I don't pay, how long am I a hostage?"

"Until I decide the debt is paid," he says simply. I close my eyes and sigh while Elliot rubs my back. "I will give you the reassurance that no one will kill you unless any of them interfere."

"Why me?" I ask, opening my eyes. "Why involve me in something I had no part of? Why not go visit my Mom in Florida and take all of that life insurance money she got?"

"I don't care about the money, Maya. It's the principle of the matter," he says.

"It has nothing to do with me," I say again, raising my voice. "I didn't ask to be born. I didn't make him run and steal your money. Fuck, I didn't even know he was Russian until today."

"Five hundred thousand in a month or a million in two," he says. "If you don't pay, I own you until I say otherwise."

"We'll get you the money," Elliot says. "How does she need to get the money to you?"

"I want it in cash," he says as he reaches into his suit jacket and pulls out a card. When I take the card, he holds onto it for a moment. "I hope you understand what will happen to you if you go to the police."

"I get it," I say as I jerk the card away from him. Nikolai chuckles and he stands with Alexi.

"Have a good evening, Maya," he says. "Remember... I see everything."

"Yeah. I hear you," I say, rolling my eyes.

We watch as they walk out of the door. After a few minutes, Arthur sighs. "They are gone."

"For now," I say.

"We can't pull off double, Dad," Elliot says.

"I know, son," he says as they all move to sit on the couch in front of the ottoman.

"How much do we have without selling off any stocks?" Elliot asks.

"About four hundred thousand," he says.

"I have an idea," Lana says. "Why don't Daniel and I take over the guest room and just sell our place?"

"What?" I ask. "No."

"That would work. You two practically live here anyway," Elliot says. "That would give plenty of room to breathe if for some reason we need to make the million."

"This is fucked up," I say. "Why is he hell-bent on taking me?"

"I feel like there is something we are missing," Brandy says. "It makes no sense to involve you."

"How much debt gets paid every time I'm raped?" I ask rhetorically.

"Maya," Elliot sighs.

"What? It's a valid question. And am I having to be raped to pay back a million or to half of that? If each rape is like twenty dollars, you may as well just move on with your life"

"I mean, that is a valid question," Lana says. "Are we

talking days? Weeks? Months? Years?"

"Shit, if it was days or weeks, I would just suffer through and save everyone some money, but months to years? No. Absolutely not," I say.

"I doubt it'll be anything short of months," Daniel says.

"Yeah," I sigh. "I need to stop thinking about this for a while."

"Well, no time like the present then," Brandy says as she sits up. "Let me see your arm."

"Mom," Elliot sighs.

"It's okay," I tell him before holding my arm out for her. She starts to take the bandage off.

"Get the first aid kit so I can rewrap this," she says as she uncovers my wrist.

"It wasn't rusted?" she asks.

"No," Elliot says. "It was new."

"Well, it's deep. I agree that it doesn't need stitches. Glue wouldn't hurt though," she says.

"Everything you need is in the kit," Elliot says as Daniel hands her the first aid kit.

I watch as she cleans it with saline solution before drying it. She applies the glue to seal it then rebandages it. "Keep it covered for a few days and it should heal just fine. Let me know if it starts getting red and I will get you some antibiotics."

"Thank you," I say.

"You are welcome dear," she says with a soft smile. "When was the last time you did this?"

"Mom," Elliot snaps.

"It's been a while. Close to a year," I say.

"And the newer ones?"

"Jonathan had a thing for doing it himself," I

say. "When hitting me wasn't enough, he'd cut me somewhere."

"Oh goodness," she says, wide-eyed.

"I'm okay though. Any time I melt down like that, I get a bit better at handling my shit," I say.

"I know you're okay," she says. "They all may be worried, but I believe you learned something valuable about your mental health today."

"Yeah," I say. "I need to be more open to letting people in. I don't have to take on everything alone just because that's what my past is like."

"Exactly," she says, smiling. "We are going to get home and start going over finances more in-depth. You all just relax for the evening."

"Have a good night," Elliot says. "I love you guys."

"We love you too, Son," Arthur says.

"I need you all to do me a favor," I say

"What?" Elliot asks.

"Don't try to find me," I say. "I know your first instinct will be to try and find a way around him to get to me, but I promise you I will be okay and I will find a way out of it myself. I walked on eggshells for twenty-five years with Dad and Jonathan... I can figure it out with Nikolai. Running from him will mean I have to do what Dad did and hide, but If I think my life is in danger, I will figure it out. Don't get killed trying to do the right thing. Be selfish and just stay put."

"Brandy and I will keep the men in line," Lana says with a smile. "Just do me a favor and make it hurt when you kill them."

"You know it," I say with a grin.

Chapter Seven

Maya

Arthur and Brandy leave so I move to lie on the couch. Elliot kisses me and they all disappear into the kitchen for a few minutes. I close my eyes and think about what is in store for me. I think I can handle it so long as he doesn't cause me any pain. I hate being in pain.

I have a feeling it will be degrading and possibly just him playing out a slave fantasy, but I can handle that. I will still kill anyone and everyone who touches me, but I can handle it. I know that I'll need to play whatever submissive role I need to so that I don't piss him off. He doesn't look very forgiving when he's mad.

Alexi is definitely going to rape me. I can just tell based on how he was looking at me. It's like I'm something he needs to break down. Jokes on him, because I will force myself into that broke girl role just so that he will think he won. I will happily play into their ego and make them think they won. I need them to not expect it when I end their life.

I get up from the couch and go to change clothes and get into something more comfortable. When I step out into the hallway, Elliot and Daniel are standing there staring at me. Lana is a bit further down the hall watching with a smirk on her face.

"Yes?" I ask slowly.

"We need to talk," Elliot says. He has the same look on his face as he did last night just before he fucked me unconscious. I glance at Lana and she just smiles.

"Alright," I say simply. I go to walk down the wall to the living room and Elliot stops and points for me to go down the hall toward the master bedroom. "Ah. It's that kind of conversation."

"Go on," he says with a smirk. We all go to the bedroom and I sit cross-legged on the end of the bed. When Daniel sits beside me and Lana stays by the room while Elliot stands in front of me, I know where this is headed.

"What is it?" I ask.

"We need to talk about what Lana told you today," he says. "I want to start by saying that I am bringing this up because I fully believe you need to get out of your head for a moment and not think about everything going on."

"I agree," I say. "I assume there are pieces of information that I am missing?"

"Massive ones," Elliot says with a smile. When Lana laughs, Elliot shakes his head at her. "That's not what I meant, Lana."

"Go on and tell her so I can know how my evening is going to play out," Lana says.

"I think I'm gathering what you are getting at," I say.

"Oh yeah?" Elliot asks.

"Considering Daniel is looking at me like he's about to attack me and you haven't hit him for it, one can assume you all are swingers," I say.

"What are your thoughts on that?" Elliot asks.

"Well, I haven't hit him either, if that answers your question," I say with a sweet smile.

Daniel turns his body to me before gently stroking the inside of my thigh. I close my eyes and take a deep breath. Having both of them look at me like this is doing something wonderful to my brain.

"Look at me," Elliot says. When I open my eyes, his eyes are filled with lust. Daniel is still touching me softly and it's starting to make me squirm, but I think that it is intentional. "No one is asking you to just go along with this."

"I know," I say.

"This is us wanting to know if it's something you want to explore with us," Elliot continues.

"I need you to be very specific and blunt as to what it is that you want me to explore," I say.

"I want Daniel and I to make you come until you can't take it anymore, and then we will fuck you," Elliot says simply.

"I want to know Lana's thoughts," I say.

"It was my idea," she says. "I am looking forward to the show."

"Does it go both ways?" I ask her.

"Meaning, would they one day do the same to me?" she asks and I nod. "Only if you're okay with it. I have no problem sharing Daniel with someone I trust, and I trust you. You are not expected to be on the same page with me on it."

"I'm open to exploring it. I can't tell you if I'm okay with it unless I am put into the position of knowing how I react," I say.

"I need a clear answer," Elliot says.

"Yes," I say. "If he is anything like you, you two are going to have to be real easy with me though."

"I will be, but I can't say the same for Daniel," Elliot

laughs. "Daniel will always wear a condom because only I will be the one getting you pregnant."

"About that…" I say.

"I know," he says. "Does it change anything we talked about?"

"No, but If I end up pregnant from rape…" I start to say.

"Then I will be here regardless of what you decide," Elliot says softly. "No matter what happens, whatever baby ends up in your belly will be my child, no matter the genetics. If you would rather have an abortion, I will hold your hand. I will always support you because it's your body."

"Okay," I smile.

"Now… Obviously, accidents happen. If for whatever reason you get pregnant and we do not know the genetics, it is up to you on how that proceeds. If you want him involved, we will both be here. The same has and always will go for Lana as well," he says.

"Is this what you want?" I ask as I turn to Daniel. The look in his eyes floors me as he slides his hand up the leg of my shorts to squeeze the bend of my hip.

"Yes, Maya," he says with a wicked smile as I whimper.

"Then show me," I say with a sweet smile.

Elliot immediately pulls my shirt off and Daniel palms my breast before teasing my nipple. "Fuck, you're gorgeous," Daniel says.

Elliot wraps his hand around my throat to have me look at him. My breath catches when he shows his first real sign of dominance. Something about his gentle hold on me and the feral look in his eyes makes my body pulsate with need as I simultaneously melt for him.

"Safeword," he says. "Choose one."

"What is Lana's?" I ask.

"Pineapple," she says.

"Then Pineapple," I say. He nods and pushes me back to lie on the bed.

Daniel takes my nipple into his mouth while sucking and nipping at me. Elliot pulls my shorts off, leaving me naked. "Dear god," I sigh and close my eyes. Elliot parts my legs wide before licking across my clit. Daniel pinches my nipple between his fingers as he nips at the other. I gasp and arch my back against his mouth.

Daniel kisses me hard right as Elliot sucks my clit into his mouth and pushes two fingers into me. His touch goes from gentle to overwhelming in an instant and it throws me head first into an orgasm. Daniel swallows my screams as my climax ripples through me. Once it fades, he still doesn't stop. He is still pounding his fingers into my body, hitting that sweet spot inside of me.

"Fuck," I moan. "Oh my God."

"Good girl, Maya," Daniel praises. "You come so pretty for us."

Another orgasm washes over me and my body feels like it's been electrocuted. I can hardly speak as he pulls a chain of orgasms out of me, each stronger than the last. Daniel is focused on teasing my nipples and it's kicking everything up a notch.

"It's too much," I whimper.

Elliot stops and pulls me up. My body feels like jello as he gets undressed and moves me to straddle him. He has me cross my injured arm across my chest before slamming into me. "Fuck!" I nearly scream. Eliott lays back and brings me with him as he starts to power fuck me from below. I am instantly reduced to moans and whimpers as he takes me.

Elliot slows and Daniel teases my ass with lubed fingers, making me groan. I am tense for a second as memories flood me of what Jonathan did. "Relax, Maya," Daniel says softly as he works my body. With each stroke, I relax more and more. "That's a good girl. Let me in, pretty girl."

He replaces his fingers with his cock and slowly slides into me. He is just as massive as Elliot and I feel stretched beyond what is physically possible. He makes small strokes into me, sinking deeper each time. In one final thrust, he fills me completely, and a guttural groan comes from my chest. They both start to move and tingles dance across my skin.

This full feeling is fucking mind-numbingly euphoric. I move up to put my weight on my uninjured arm and keep the other on Elliot's chest. They are both gripping me tightly as they fuck me.

"God, it feels so good," I whimper.

"You like our cocks buried in you, baby girl?" Daniel asks as he pulls me up completely. He wraps his arms around my waist and I lay my head back on his shoulder. One of them starts to rub my clit and I moan loudly as another orgasm punches through me. Daniel bites my neck and everything intensifies.

"Fuck fuck fuck. Oh my God. Oh God, please. Harder," I beg. They both turn frenzied as they start slamming into me with more force. My next orgasm causes my entire body to tense and my scream to get caught as I drag them both down with me.

I am completely catatonic by the time they move me to lie on the bed to clean and dress me. I have no energy left in me, so I fall asleep.

Chapter Eight

One month later

It's been one month today since Nikolai demanded I pay up or get taken. We have basically all of the money in cash. Daniel and Lana are selling their house today for cash, so we should have the rest of the money gathered in the next hour. They left me at the house after having a complete meltdown.

I'm a week late for my period, so Lana convinced me to take a test. Lo and behold... I'm pregnant. Knowing that Nikolai wants to steal me, I was suddenly overwhelmed and broke down. I am excited to have a baby with Elliot. We have talked a lot over the last month about it, but I am so fucking scared for my baby right now. What if their assaults cause me to lose the baby? What if I'm gone for long enough and they take them from me? There are so many bad things that could happen, but hopefully, the sale of this house will solve all the problems.

As soon as Elliot texts me to tell me they have cash in hand I am going to text the number on the card to find out where I am meeting him. I've been moving around since they left the house. I can't sit still because I'm afraid I will implode if I do.

I've cleaned the entire house, including putting everyone's clothes away. They hate it when I do this but

I'm so used to keeping a house that it is only natural for me to want to continue that. When I'm stressed out, I clean. Right now, I am far past stressed.

When my phone goes off, I quickly pull it out to see that Elliot has texted me.

Elliot: Cash in hand. Text him. I love you.

Me: Thank God! I love you too. Texting now.

I go to the kitchen to get the card and text the number on it.

Me: I have the money. Where do I take it?

Unknown: Stay put. We will come to you.

Fuck. What if Elliot isn't here when they get here? I'll be alone with them. What happens when they get here and I don't actually have the money with me? Would they actually wait?

Me: They told me to stay put, and they would come to me. You need to hurry.

Elliot: Fuck. We are an hour out. Don't let anyone in until I get there.

Me: I love you so much, Elliot...

Now I am panicking. Who knows how long it will take them to get here? It could be in five minutes or six hours. I am pacing the house, trying to keep myself calm.

It's only been ten minutes when I hear a car door shut outside. I run to the door and lock it. I know it won't keep them out but maybe it will hold them off for a second.

There is a knock at the door, but I ignore it. They keep knocking and my phone goes off for a text.

Unknown: Open the door, Maya.

Me: Elliot is on his way. I'll open it when he gets here.

Unknown: So you don't have it?

Me: Elliot is on his way.

Unknown: Wrong answer.

Right as the message comes through, a kick slams the door open, and in walks Nikolai with two men behind him. I recognize one of them, but not the other.

"Hello, Maya," he says with a sickening smile. "Where is it?"

"E-Elliot has it. He's on his way," I say as I back up.

"So you don't have it?" he asks.

"We have it. You'll get it when he gets here," I say hurriedly. When I take another step back, I run into someone. They tightly grip my waist and I freeze.

"The one-month mark passed twenty minutes ago, Igrushka," Alexi says in my ear. "That makes it double."

"Do you have double?" Nikolai asks as he closes in on me, leaving no room between us.

"Elliot will be here soon," I say as tears roll down my cheeks.

I'm so fucked. They're about to take me. I just know it. We don't have double. There is no way we could find double.

"Answer the question," Nikolai asks as he roughly grabs my chin and forces me to look up at him.

"No," I whimper. "You never said it was to the

minute. We have five hundred thousand."

"Oh, sweet Igrushka," Nikolai tuts at me. "You know now, don't you?"

"Please don't do this," I cry. "You gave me two months. We will get the rest."

"I've changed my mind," he says with a grin. "Bring her to the car, Alexi." He turns and walks away.

"*No. Please don't,*" I scream and try to move away from Alexi. He swiftly grabs me by the hair and yanks me back to him. When I'm close, he spins me and throws me over his shoulder with little effort. "*Stop. Please stop.*" I immediately fall into hysterics, kicking and hitting Alexi, trying to get him to let me go.

He carries me to the driveway before setting me on my feet. Before I can hit him again he grabs me by the throat and slams me against the car. "Are you going to be good?" he asks. "Because if not, I will be more than happy to punish you." He is squeezing my throat so I just nod. When he lets me go, I refrain from hitting him again.

Alexi opens the door to the car and points. "Get in," he says.

"Please don't do this," I beg.

"Get in the goddamn car or I'll fuck you right here in front of that doorbell camera," he growls in my ear. "Do you want Elliot to see how you are going to scream for me?"

My shoulders slump in defeat and I get into the car. Nikolai grabs my arm and pulls me to the center so Alexi can get in. The man in the driver seat simply puts the car in reverse and drives away like he didn't just help kidnap me.

I stay drawn into myself as he drives. I still pay attention to where we are going. I may be overwhelmed with emotion right now, but my head is clear enough to know that I need to pay attention.

Nikolai and Alexi are watching me closely. Occasionally they will glance at each other, but I refuse to look up at either of them. "You are quiet, Igrushka," Nikolai says. I ignore him to avoid letting my anger out. He doesn't like being ignored, so he grabs my face and turns to look at him. "When I speak to you, you answer. Understand, Igrushka?"

"Yes," I say, seething.

"That is 'yes sir' to you," he says.

"Yes sir," I say, correcting myself. I'm not trying to get hit by this man.

"Do you have any questions?" he asks.

"How long?" I ask.

"How long?" he questions back.

"How long do I have to be with you?" I ask.

"Until you birth the child I'm going to put in your belly," he says before kissing my cheek.

Fuck. This is bad. This is more than bad. I'm stuck with him. He will figure out eventually that I'm pregnant. I'm early, so I'll be able to hide it for a while. I can at least say that I just had a period so it will buy me at least a month.

"You're sick," I say with a shaky voice.

"The sooner you get pregnant and have my child, the sooner you get to leave. I expect you to learn to be compliant," he says. "I will be forgiving once, but otherwise you will be punished if you try to deny me. The others you may fight as you see fit."

"Oh, I encourage you to fight me," Alexi says happily, squeezing my thigh.

"Everyone who touches you will wear a condom. If

they don't, you are to tell me immediately. Okay?" he asks.

"Yes sir," I say

"And lastly, if you are good... you get to be in your own room. If you are not, you will be chained to a bed in the basement."

"What will I be doing?" I ask quietly. "Besides being raped."

"You'll be with my housekeeper. She will give you a list of things to do. When those are done you are free to do anything but leave or contact anyone," he says.

"I can read?" I ask.

"Yes. As long as you are good, I'll have someone bring you a Kindle," he says. I simply nod and say nothing further. "Now... Show me how thankful you are that I'm being kind."

I stare at him in disbelief. I know what he means, but my brain is slow to process. He wants it to seem as though I am willingly choosing to blow him.

"It's either you show your thanks or Ivan pulls over and all four of us take our turn with you," he says with a smile. "Make your decision. Be advised that Ivan likes to make it hurt."

"Okay," I whisper. "Okay."

Nikolai lets go of my face and I close my eyes for a moment to center my thoughts. This is fucking ridiculous. All of this is because Jonathan got his feelings hurt. I want to blame myself and say I shouldn't have left him, but I meant it when I told him I'd rather be raped by Nikolai than be with Jonathan.

Nikolai doesn't seem like he wants to hit me or hurt me. I'm sure he will if I push him, but I have no intention of doing that. I might have an issue with not being a smartass to Alexi though. Everything about him pisses me off. His stupid fucking smile enrages me.

"I won't repeat myself, Igrushka," he coos.

"Fuck," I sigh. "Alright."

I turn in my seat to face Nikolai but not to meet his eyes. He suddenly grabs me by the throat and forces me to look up at him. "If I feel any teeth... I'll gut you myself. Got it?"

"Yes sir," I say softly. He releases me and I divert my eyes down to break eye contact with him. I hesitate for a moment but force myself to move my hands to his belt. When I pull him free of his pants he is fully erect. I'm not a violent person but this situation is changing that rapidly. It's taking everything in me to not break his dick, but I know he meant it when he said he would gut me.

"Don't be shy. We both know you know how to suck cock," Nikolai says with humor in his tone. I keep all of my disparaging, small-dick comments to myself. I'd love to hurt his ego, even though he's definitely not small. I wouldn't be that lucky.

I take him in my mouth and he groans as he fists my hair. He doesn't directly force himself down my throat but he applies enough pressure to the back of my head that I know he's giving me the option to choose or choke. I choose to take him to the back of my throat and give him what he wants. He keeps a tight grip on my hair as I bob up and down on him. I do my best to get him to finish quickly so this can be over with. I suck him down harder when he moans. He's close and I need this to end quickly. He groans once more and forces himself down my throat as he comes, making me swallow his load.

When he puts himself back in his pants he grabs my face and pulls me close to him. I realize I have tears rolling down my cheeks. So much for trying to be strong.

I need to stay calm because I can't melt down. My baby needs me to push through this and get them back to safety. Elliot will take care of us, we just need to get to him.

"Good girl, Igrushka," he says before licking across my lips. I fight the urge to recoil with a gag when he licks the remnants of his fluids off my mouth.

"What does that mean?" I ask.

"It means toy," he says with a smile. "Because you're mine to play with... and mine to break." The car comes to a stop and he lets go of my face. "Take her to her room. Maria should have her clothes already in there."

"No problem," Alexi says. "We will have fun, won't we Maya?" He squeezes my thigh and I wince at the aggressiveness.

"Wear a condom," Nikolai says as he opens his door and gets out. I don't move because Alexi still has a tight grip on my thigh.

"Are you going to be a brat? I'd like to not take you to the basement but I will if you are going to fight me," he says.

"I won't be a brat," I say flatly.

"Good," he says. "Let's go see your new room."

Alexi gets out and pulls me with him. The house is massive and stark white. The lawn is perfectly manicured and the flower beds with flawlessly shaped topiary bushes. It's a beautiful home, but it houses the devil.

Alexi takes me inside and leads me upstairs to the end of a hallway. When we walk into the room, it's far nicer than I expected. There is a massive king-sized bed centered under a window. There is a skimpy maid outfit lying on the end of the bed next to a Kindle.

"You'll wear that every day. At night you can wear

whatever else is in the closet," Alexi says before turning to me and winking. "No need for panties."

I roll my eyes without thinking and he grabs me by the throat and pulls me against his chest. "I'm sorry," I whisper.

"Get changed," he says. "Lose the attitude or you'll be punished."

He pushes me backward and I sniff back my tears. "Please don't," I cry.

"What's wrong, Maya? You acted so bravely the last time I saw you," Alexi says as he backs me against the end of the bed. "Get naked and put the dress on. Now."

I hesitate and Alexi moves in such a way that I think he's about to hit me. I recoil with a gasp and nearly fall into the bed. His movements trigger me to comply immediately and I start undressing. I don't want to get hit, so I just do as I am told.

Alexi steps back and watches as I take all of my clothes off. I quickly put on the dress and it hardly covers my ass. Alexi steps closer to me and roughly squeezes my ass with both hands. When he presses me against his body, he presses his erection against my belly. More tears fall when he grins at me.

He moves his hand up to fist my hair before jerking my head back. He kisses and bites my neck and chest while I try to not openly sob. I'm trying to keep control over my emotions but when he spins me around and bends me over the bed, I lose it. I instinctively try to fight but he plants his hand between my shoulder blades to pin me in place.

I am crying so hard that I can't form any comprehendible words. I hear the condom wrapper open and I try to relax myself so he doesn't hurt me. Alexi tightly holds my hips and I prepare for him to slam into me but he slowly slides into me. It throws me so far off that my body responds in a way I don't expect and I groan.

"That's right, little whore," he groans in my ear.

"Please stop," I beg and he slowly pumps into me. He's big and based on how he is groaning, he likes the way my body is responding to him. I try to make it stop but he pushes in deeper and forces a moan from me.

"You're going to come for me Maya," he says as he pulls out of me and rolls me to my back.

"Please stop," I repeat.

Alexi wraps his hand around my throat and lightly squeezes. The other hand travels to my clit to tease it before slamming himself into me. All of the feelings combine at once and I gasp and arch my back. He takes this as his cue to pound into me harder, playing on the sensations he's already built. My body may be responding to him exactly the way he intends, but I am still sobbing through the moans.

Something about the way he pulls this orgasm forward is painful and icky. It feels wrong, as if my body *knows* it's wrong but it just can't help itself. I try to focus my thoughts on anything but the way he is pinching and rolling my clit as he steadily slams against my g-spot.

"Come on my cock, whore," he growls.

"I won't," I force out through a moan.

"Come for me like your slut mother did for Nikolai. It's in your blood to fuck," he says as he strokes into me. He pinches my clit harder. I feel my body starting to unravel but his words in my ear stun me. "When he's deep inside of you, remember to call him daddy."

Before I can process what he has said, an orgasm punches through me and I groan as the weak ripples move through my belly. Alexi moans in my ear as he sinks into me and comes. He gets off me and leaves and goes to the door. I am still lying on the bed crying, not willing to get up.

"Collect yourself and come downstairs," Alexi says. "Thirty minutes or I send Ivan up here."

"Alexi," I say as I sit up.

"Yes, Maya?" he turns and smirks at me.

"I don't care if it is the last thing I do... I will be the last thing you see before you die." I say seriously.

"We'll see about that," he chuckles and walks out of the room, shutting the door behind him.

I get up and run to the bathroom when a wave of nausea hit me. I hardly make it before I vomit. When my stomach stops torturing me, I clean up and go downstairs.

Chapter Nine

Elliot

I throw the car into park before jumping out. The front door is wide open and I know. I know when I walk into that house, Maya will be gone. I shouldn't have left her alone today. Nikolai texted and said one month has passed and the price was now double but didn't say that he took her. Not that I thought he would.

I run into the house calling out for Maya, searching every room. She's gone. Her phone is on the living room floor and the door is busted open. I pick it up and read through the messages with Nikolai and it confirms my suspicions. He took her.

"*Fuck!*" I scream. I grip her phone in my hand, talking myself down from losing my temper.

"Oh no," Lana says as she starts to tear up. "She's gone."

"I'm going to fucking kill him," Daniel growls. He goes to move to the door and Lana bolts to get in front of him before he can get out of the door.

"We promised her, Dan," Lana sniffs.

"We can't just fucking sit here while they rape her, Lana," he says, raising his voice.

"I know, baby. I know," she says. "We promised her we'd trust her. We need to let her do this because it will destroy you if she gets killed because we tried to get to her."

"She's right." I say with a sigh.

"Of all people, you should want to get to her," Daniel snaps at me.

"You don't think I want to kill that fucker, Daniel? I want to break his fucking neck, but I trust she knows what she's doing," I say. "That woman has been through more in her life than we will ever realize. She can handle this because she is strong and she's smart. We need to talk to her Mom and see if we can find out any information about Nikolai."

"Fine," he huffs.

I start searching through her contacts until I find her mom's name. Michelle Sparks. It takes her a second to answer, but she does.

"Hello," she says with a sigh.

"Michelle? My name is Elliot Greene. I am seeing Maya," I say.

"Is something wrong?" she asks.

"Yes. Her ex told Nikolai Pavlov who her father is and he kidnapped her today," I say. "Can you tell me anything about him?"

"I uh… I'm sorry. I can't help… I'm so sorry," she says as take abruptly hangs up.

"What the fuck," I say, shocked.

"Did she just hang up on you?" Lana asked.

"Yeah," I say. "What kind of fucking parents does Maya have?"

"Awful ones," Lana frowns.

"What the fuck do we do now?" Daniel says.

"Research, for now. I'll only be patient for so long," I say.

For the rest of the day, we look up everything

we can about Maya's family in connection with Nikolai Pavlov.

Everything feels wrong without Maya being here. She'd be sitting in my lap watching me work with her head laid on my chest right now. She'd make jokes and be playful when she got bored. When she got needy, she'd turn and straddle me to let me know exactly what she wanted.

Fuck, I miss the way she blushes when I compliment her. She smiles so brightly and her cheeks down to her chest, turn a cute shade of pink when she gets all sheepish about me calling her beautiful. She is though. She is the most beautiful woman I have ever met, inside and out. In everything she does, she considers everyone around her first. Her kind nature is the most stunning thing about her.

I won't deny that just the memory of her little whimpers before she comes does something to me. I love the way her eyes roll back and she clings to me just before she loses control. Everything about her is fucking mesmerizing.

I miss her so much it hurts. I just saw her this morning, but it feels like it's been days. I know I need to trust her, but all I want to do is save her.

Chapter Ten

Maya

I get downstairs and stay at the bottom of the landing until someone notices me. I don't want to be seen or heard, so I'm just going to stay out of everyone's way. Nikolai and Alexi are talking in Russian and haven't noticed me. I hear my name a few times, so I know they are discussing me.

I knew they would degrade me, but a slutty maid's dress? They couldn't come up with anything more original? By Alexi saying I can't wear underwear, I assume that means I'll be assaulted often enough that underwear won't matter.

I'm so afraid of losing the baby because of the assaults. As long as they don't use foreign objects or go too hard, I'm sure I'll be okay. I have to make sure that I keep it a secret for as long as possible.

The fact that Nikolai might be my biological father and he made me blow him makes me want to throw up again. Too much stress has always made me get sick, so if I end up with morning sickness, I can blame it on that. Hopefully, I can manage to get out of here before then. God forbid he finds out I'm pregnant, he will likely abort it.

"Maya, come sit so we can talk," Nokiali says. I move closer and sit on the couch, opposite him and Alexi. "How do you like your room?"

"It's nice. Thank you," I say quietly.

"Are there any feminine products you may need soon?" he asks.

"No. Not right now," I say. It's not a lie. I don't need them right now.

"Maria is my housekeeper and she is also a nurse. She will be checking you over to make sure you are healthy enough to carry a child," he says.

"And if I'm not?" I ask.

"Then you are of no use to me," he says.

"She will draw blood and give you a pregnancy test," he says.

"No," I snap and immediately shut my mouth.

"No?" he asks, raising an eyebrow.

"I'm sorry. I'm just a little weirded out by needles," I lie.

"Ah. Well, I will let her make the judgment if bloodwork is needed. Deal?", he asks.

"Yes. Thank you," I say.

"Maria," he calls out.

"Yes sir?" A woman says when she comes into the room. She is in her mid-thirties and beautiful.

"Take Maya and go over her medical history and administer a pregnancy test," Nikolai says. "If you need blood work, she will comply."

"Yes sir," she says. She motions for me to follow her. I follow her and try to fight back the tears. I should have known he'd want to see if I am healthy or not.

We get to a room that looks almost like an exam room. Tears are slowly sliding down my face.

"How'd you end up here?" she asks.

"My dad used to work for him. When he bolted, he

stole from him," I say.

"Who is your dad?"

"Armen," I say.

"His brother?" Maria asks.

"What? My dad was an orphan," I say.

"Yeah, their middle brother was dropped off at an orphanage in Russia when he was born because their parents didn't have any money to feed him. He ended up in the States and remained there in a home. Nikolai and Alexi found him thirty years ago. He ran away five years later and stole fifty thousand dollars from him," she says.

"Fifty?" I ask. That son of a bitch. He was never going to take the money. He was just fucking with me.

"Yeah. Why are you crying?" she asks. I shake my head and she narrows her eyes. "Are you not healthy? He won't kill you if you're sick."

"It's not that," I whisper.

"Then what is it? I won't help you escape, but I'll keep you alive the best I can. He trusts me," she says.

"Why do you want to help me?" I ask.

"Because I don't agree with him raping someone until they give him a child," she says. "It's low, even for him."

"I'm already pregnant," I say.

"Oh fuck," she gasps. "That's bad. How far along?"

"I just found out before he took me. No more than five weeks. Maybe less," I say, wiping my tears.

"How about this? I'll fake the test and buy you a month until he notices that you haven't had a cycle. I'll have to disclose it then but I can buy you some time by making him think it's his."

"O-okay," I whimper.

"You need to get out of here when you can," she

says. "I'll throw you under the bus so fast to save myself, but I'll do what I can to keep you alive as long as it doesn't hurt me."

"Thank you," I sniff

She soaks the test in water to get it to show negative while we sit in silence. After a while, she takes me back to Nikolai.

"She's healthy and just ended her cycle. She will be ovulating in two weeks, give or take a few days," she says.

"Wonderful. Thank you," Nikolai says. "She will be helping you every day. Just tell her what you want her to do. Don't overload her."

"I'll just have her clean the bedrooms," Maria says. That's the trade-off for helping me, I guess. I have to go into people's bedrooms. I wonder how often she is raped? I wouldn't blame her for wanting a break from that. If she's gained his trust, she likely has some sort of freedom. She turns to me to continue. "You'll make the beds and wash anything that needs washing, sheets included. They all have hardwood floors, so you'll sweep and lightly clean the floors. Once a week they will need to be mopped. The ones that have bathrooms are pretty tidy, so just wipe things down as needed. Tomorrow I'll show you where everything is."

"Okay. Thank you," I say.

"Is Maya allowed to interact with me?" Maria asks.

"So long as you remember what will happen if you break my rules. Maya understands what will happen to her if she tries to leave," Nikolai says.

"Yes sir. Thank you. I feel she will be far more compliant if she's not bored."

"I agree," Nikolai says before turning to me. "Come with me."

"Yes sir," I say quietly.

"I'm going to show her the basement," he tells Alexi.

"Have fun," Alexi says with a grin. Fear shoots through me as I follow him. I feel like I'm walking myself to my own beating right now. We walk down into the basement and it is a plain concrete room with an iron bed bolted to the floor in one corner is a Saint Andrew's cross with a wooden chest beside it.

"Are you going to fight me?" he asks as he points for me to sit on the bed.

"I don't know," I say honestly. I do as I say because I'd rather be in the bed than strapped to that cross.

"It's either you will or you won't," he frowns and moves to stand directly in front of me.

"No, it's not, Nikolai. I have spent my entire life being hurt by other people. I have PTSD and I can't tell you I will comply because I also told myself I would never cut myself again. You threatened me and the very first thing I did was spiral and try to kill myself. So no, it's not yes or no. Add in awful and debilitating mental health issues, and I promise you won't want to hand shit down to them. If you want your kid to be fucked up, by all means. Get someone who might not be your biological daughter pregnant."

"Who said I might be your father? Your Mom?"

"No. Alexi did. He commented on it when he raped me," I say bluntly.

"What did he say?" he asks. He takes a step back from me and I can see worry in his eyes.

"He said come for me like your slut mother did for Nikolai. It's in your blood to fuck. Then told me to remember when you're inside me to call you Daddy," I explain.

Nikolai backs away from me and looks like he's in shock. "Go to your room and change. You can put on something from the closet or what you had on, but do not come out of that room until I come to get you. Got it?"

"Yes sir," I say, confused. He seriously is freaking out over this. I turn to go to the door and he stops me.

"Maya," he says.

"Yes?"

"If you're my daughter, I will make up for this," he says. "If anyone tries to touch you, tell them I have forbidden it. Including Alexi."

"Okay," I say. I practically run up the stairs and through the kitchen. When I round the corner I slam into Alexi.

"Where are you going?" he asks, grabbing my arm to stop me.

"Nikolai told me to go to my room," I say.

"Let's go then," he says with a sickening smile.

"He said everyone is forbidden from touching me and I was told to say that if anyone tried, including you," I say as I jerk my arm out of his grip.

"Go, Maya. I'll come up after a while to talk to you," he says in a much softer tone than I've heard from him yet.

"Yes sir," I say as I leave the kitchen and go upstairs. When I get into the room I immediately change back into the clothes I was wearing and sit on the bed. I can hear Nikolai screaming at Alexi in Russian.

This whole situation just got really weird. I don't know what is going on but Nikolai looked mortified when I told him I might be his daughter.

It would make sense. We have the same hair and

eye color. I look nothing like Armen, but I do Nikolai. Seeing as though he is okay with rape, just not his daughter. The more I think about it, the more I realize that there is a good chance that Nikolai is my biological father.

Chapter Eleven

Elliot

I am woken suddenly by Lana smacking my arm. "What!" I snap.

"It's Nikolai," she says, placing a phone into my hand. I sit up off the couch and take the phone.

"Hello?" I say as I place the call on speakerphone as Daniel and Lana sit beside me.

"Elliot. I'm going to send you an address. I need you to come get Maya," he says.

"What happened? What did you do to her?" I ask.

"She's fine. Just go to the address. It's my house," he says.

"I'm not dumb enough to walk into a trap," I say bluntly.

"It's not a trap. Bring the others if you want. Just come get her. She'll be expecting you," he says.

"I need to know what's going on, Nikolai. You break in and kidnap her and now you're releasing her?"

"I was informed today by her and Alexi that there is a high probability that Maya is my daughter," he says.

"We called her mother about it and she hung up on us immediately," I say.

"Right. So come get her, Elliot," he says. "Whatever debt was owed is resolved."

"Okay. Send me the address and I'll be there soon," I

say as I stand up.

"I will bring her out to you to limit her interaction with Alexi," he says.

"Is she hurt?" I ask.

"Physically she's fine. Alexi did rape her though. He made a comment to her that basically told her about me being her father. She told me and Alexi, then confirmed that I am. Her birthday lines up, so I'm almost certain that she is," he explains.

"Did you rape her?" I ask.

"Not in the sense you're thinking," he says.

"But something happened?" I ask.

"Yes. She can explain," he says. "I'll be keeping an eye out." I end the call and we all run to the car. As soon as I get the car, a text comes through with an address.

Chapter Twelve

Maya

I've been sitting here for a while now. Nikolai and Alexi have stopped yelling. Everything went silent about twenty minutes ago.

The bedroom door swings open and I jump up from the bed and back away as Nikolai comes in. He looks angry.

"Come on," he says motioning for me to come with him. I hesitate and he sighs. "Elliot is here, Maya. Come on."

"What? Why? I told him not to do anything dumb. I swear to god," I say as I start to panic. I told him and he promised. They all promised.

"Relax, Maya. I called him," he says. "Let's get you to him and we will talk more."

"O-okay," I say. He motions for me to exit the room again and this time I comply. When I step out of the room, Alexi is glaring at me.

"I'll be seeing you, Maya," he says with that same stupid grin. Behind that smile is rage though. You can see it in his eyes. When Nikolai says something to him in Russian, that anger slips out a bit more.

I stop when I get to the front door because I don't know if I'm allowed to just... walk out.

"Go on," Nikolai says as he opens the door.

When I step out and see Elliot, I take off running to him. He catches me in a hug and I wrap my legs around him as he squeezes me tightly. A flood of tears overwhelms me and he sets me on my feet to cup my face.

"Are you okay? Are you hurt?" Elliot asks softly.

"I'm okay," I say as I wipe my tears. Elliot kisses me softly before pointing behind me. I turn and Daniel pulls me towards him to hug me.

"Are you sure you're okay?" Daniel asks as he wipes away my tears.

"I'm sure. I'm okay," I say again. When I see Lana, I start crying again when she puts her arms around me.

"Thank you for coming," I say.

"You're my best friend, Maya. I'll always be here," she says sweetly. She turns to look at Nikolai and glares at him.

"Maya," Nikolai says. I turn to face him but Elliot pulls me to stand between him and Daniel.

"Alexi is your brother?" I ask.

"Yes. He is the youngest. Your father was the middle," he says.

"Maria told me," I say.

"I figured she would," he says. "Look…"

"If you are looking to make amends for what you did today, you're not getting it," I say simply.

"I know, but we need to be sure," Nikolai says. "I need you to go to a lab tomorrow and have blood work done. They will expedite the test."

"Every time you speak, it's a trap. You failed to say that the one-month deadline was to the minute, then I find out that my father only stole fifty thousand from you. All of that was just a ploy to get me here; to fuck with my head before you locked me in your house to try and get me pregnant," I say, feeling safe enough now to speak freely. "If that test comes back that Alexi was wrong, what then? The truth this time."

"The debt has been resolved," he says.

"Oh, because I was raped by my uncle? No matter how you look at it, I was raped by my uncle. Also, you may have very well made your own biological daughter blow you. If not your daughter... your niece. Now you want to act guilty because you were *seconds* away from raping me when I told you that you were about to forcefully fuck your own daughter... But your niece is okay? Getting your niece pregnant is okay, but not your daughter? It's refreshing to know where that line of morality sits with you, Nikolai," I say, raising my voice.

"Maya," he says with a sigh.

"Save it, Nikolai," I snap. "I will go and get the fucking blood work but understand that I will be your undoing. I will make it my life's mission to be the last thing on your mind, plaguing your thoughts, when you die. I will pray to God each and every fucking night that you die alone and miserable. I will burn your fucking empire to the ground and rebuild my life in its ashes. Fuck you and this fucking family."

I am shaking with rage when I finally get myself to shut up. Luckily, Nikolai doesn't appear to be mad or irritated in the least at my threat.

"Do you know the lab on Barlow Street?" he asks Elliot.

"Yeah. I'll take her there tomorrow if she wants," Elliot says simply.

"Alright. I will have them call you and tell you the results," Nikolai says to me.

"So that'll be my heads-up that we start this

bullshit all over?" I ask bitterly. "Will you show up again twenty minutes after the call?"

"I know you don't believe me, Maya, but it's done," he says. "I will not come after you for any reason."

"And Alexi?" I ask.

"I'll handle Alexi," he says.

"If you don't," Daniel says. "I will."

"Let's go," Elliot says to me.

I walk to the car with Elliot, Daniel, and Lana. I sit in the passenger seat next to Elliot and Nikolai watches as Elliot drives us all away from the house of horrors. We ride in silence for a while. Elliot is tightly gripping my hand as if it will all just be a dream if he lets go of me. I still feel like this is a trap somehow, but I will try to not worry myself to death over it. At this point, I should start reducing stress for the sake of the baby.

I haven't told Elliot that I'm pregnant. Lana knows, but I doubt she said anything. Elliot would have lost this shit and tried to save me. When we get to the house, I will tell him. Right now I just want to enjoy the silence. I spent hours listening to Nikolai and Alexi take turns screaming at one another in Russian, so the silence is needed.

When we get home, I flop down on the couch. "The door is fixed," I say.

"Yeah, Daniel fixed it while Elliot was forcing himself to not leave the house," Lana says.

"So they don't know?" I ask.

"They do not," she says with a bright smile.

"Know what?" Elliot asks as he pulls me up to stand. I smile at Lana and she giggles.

"Remember how I freaked the fuck out this morning?" I ask.

"Yeah," he says slowly.

"I never told you what was wrong," I say.

"I assume you will tell me now?" he asks.

"Yeah," I say as I take his hands into mine. He looks nervous but when I smile at him, he relaxes. "I am a week late, so Lana went out and bought a test."

"You're killing me, Baby," he says impatiently.

"I'm pregnant, Elliot," I say sweetly. "I freaked out before dipshit was still after me. Apparently, my intuition was spot on."

Elliot wraps me in a hug and he is quickly overcome with emotion. I know all of the "what if" situations are running rampant in his mind right now. We are both stuck between excitement and fear. Excitement to bring our baby into this world, but the fear of Nikolai and Alexi nearly consume the dreams for our little family.

"I love you," he says as he pulls away and cups my face. "I don't know what to say right now other than I love you."

"That's more than enough, Elliot," I say as I go up on my tip-toes to kiss him.

"At least we will save money on condoms," Daniel says. Elliot and I laugh.

"Naturally you'd say that," I say, laughing.

"Congratulations, Maya. You are already a great mom," Daniel says as he hugs me.

"Thank you," I say softly as he hugs me. The way he is holding me. I can tell that he is overwhelmed with emotion now. He has no plans of letting me go anytime soon.

"Elliot is insufferable without you," Daniel says before kissing my neck and pulling away to look at me.

"I was gone for less than a day, Daniel," I say.

"They were *both* insufferable," Lana says. "I'm

stealing Maya so she can take a bath and relax."

She takes my hand and pulls me away from the guys. When we get to the master bathroom she starts filling the clawfoot bathtub.

"Are you actually okay? No cramping or anything?" she asks.

"Yeah, I'm okay. Alexi wasn't violent, just degrading," I say. "Is it bad that I don't feel traumatized? Like... It sucks that it happened and it makes me angry, but it doesn't hurt. Ya know?"

"You are desensitized to trauma at this point, I'm sure," she says. "No one is required to act a certain way with trauma. You are traumatized, it's just affecting you differently than it would someone else."

"He made me come," I say bluntly. "That's fucked up, right? Like..."

"No. Stop right there. You didn't ask for any of that, so how your body responds is beyond your control. Let's just be thankful he didn't do any damage and you are home now," she says. "Get undressed and get in."

I nod and undress. When I step into the water and sit, I groan at how the warmth envelops me. I didn't realize just how much I needed this. When I look at Lana I watch as she drags her eyes over my body. She has lust in her eyes and it triggers a fantasy in my mind. Thinking about her touching me feels natural.

I've never really put much thought into whether I am bi or not. Seeing the way she looks at me makes me wonder what it would be like to be the one to make her come. Would she be better than the guys at getting me off because she is a woman?

When her eyes meet mine, we are sharing the same desires. She wants to touch me and I want to find out how good it will feel to come for my best friend. "Do you care to help me wash my back?" I ask.

"I can do that," she says with a sweet smile. "Sit up."

I sit up and she starts to undress. I watch her intently while she watches my reaction to her body. She's fucking gorgeous. Everything about her is perfect. I don't know if it's a trauma response or if this is a bi-awakening for me, but all I want is for her to get in this bath with me and take my mind off things for a second.

She steps into the bath and sits behind me before grabbing the washcloth and slowly washing my back. Her touch is gentle and every time she softly drags her fingers down my back I bite back a whimper. Her touch is growing to be more intentional in the way she glides her hands down my sides to my hip before rubbing up the center of my back with her thumbs pressed into either side of my spine. I close my eyes and sigh as she massages my back. Her hands on my skin are both erotic and tranquilizing.

I am fully aware of Elliot and Daniel standing in the doorway of the bathroom. When she kisses my shoulder, the guys easily slip out of my thoughts. Her kisses are soft and feather-light as they move to my neck. Lana pulls me back to lie against her chest.

"We have an audience," she whispers in my ear.

"Yeah, it's because they're perverts," I say with a smile, keeping my eyes closed.

"How long have you thought you were bi?" she asks.

"About five minutes," I laugh.

"Are you seeking comfort or is something else going through your head?"

"Something else," I admit.

"Concerns?" she asks.

"That I'm wrong and it's a trauma response," I admit.

"Because you think it will ruin our friendship if you're wrong," she asks.

"Yeah."

"Maya, if comfort is what you need, I'll be your comfort," she says before whispering in my ear. "Either way, they are about to watch me make you come."

Lana moves to palm my breasts and gently squeeze before teasing my nipples, making me sigh and relax into her more. She starts kissing, nipping, and licking my neck as her hand slides down my body. I gasp softly and arch slightly when she rubs across my clit.

"That feels nice." I sigh. She responds by rubbing me in small circles. Her touch is perfect. The way she is touching me makes my breathing accelerate. I grip the sides of the bathtub as pleasure starts to bubble up inside of me.

"Every little sound you make is fucking amazing," she says.

"Fuck, that feels incredible, Lana," I moan.

She moves her hand from my breast to turn my face to her and she kisses me. I immediately bring my hands to her face and deepen our kiss. She picks up speed and I moan loudly against her mouth. She tastes like heaven as our tongues explore a new side of our friendship.

When I can no longer focus on kissing her, I lie my head back on her shoulder and grip the tub again. "Fuck, Lana," I moan.

"Come for us, Maya," she says softly. "Show me how much you like the way I touch you."

"I'm so close," I whimper.

"Relax, Maya," she urges. When I willingly relax my body an orgasm rushes my body and I moan loudly as I arch my back. She pulls every little whimper out of me before pulling her hand away from me.

The intensity of my climax allows the trauma to sink into my brain and so I start crying. Lana wraps her arms around me and holds me while I cry.

"Maya," she says softly.

"I didn't want it to happen, but it did," I whimper through my tears.

"Can I ask you something?" she asks.

"Yeah," I sniff.

"What was the difference between that and what you felt when he raped you?" she asks.

"It hurt with him," I say quietly.

"Did I hurt you, Maya?" she asks.

"No, you didn't," I admit.

"That's the difference between consent, and non-consent, Maya," she says. "Your body is going to respond regardless, but when you want it, you enjoy it. When you don't, it causes discomfort. Your brain knows you don't want it, but your body still has a job to do. You cannot blame yourself for something your body was made to do. Blame him for taking advantage of those biological factors."

"Thank you," I say as I wipe my face.

"For making you come or for showing you the difference?" she asks.

"The difference," I laugh.

When I open my eyes Elliot and Daniel look feral. I smile sweetly at them as Elliot walks closer to offer me his hand. When I take it, he stands me up out of the bath before lifting me and setting me down in front of him.

"Hi," I say with a smile.

Daniel steps closer and pulls Lana up from the bath and sets her next to me.

"That is not what I expected to walk into," Elliot says.

"Did you enjoy the show?" I ask.

"You're both about to find out how much," Daniel says seriously.

"You think?" I ask, challenging him.

He holds his hand out with a smile. When I take it he pulls me out of the bathroom with Elliot bringing Lana in. "I need an honest answer, Maya. Are you okay? No pain?" Daniel asks as he cups my face.

"No pain," I say with a smile. "I'm okay. I promise."

"Was that for comfort or are you wanting to explore things with Lana?" he asks.

"I want to explore things," I say.

"Okay," he says. "We are all three going to overwhelm you to help get your mind off things. You get stuck in your head too easily and clearly, we have found a way to help you out of a spiral. We all know it's inevitable that the emotions will hit you."

"Do I finally get to experience you leading, Daniel?" I ask sweetly.

"Do you want me to lead, Maya?"

"Yes please!" I say happily.

Daniel smiles at me as he pulls his shirt off. I watch him completely undress before he grabs the back of my thighs and picks me up. "After watching my wife make you come, I don't have the willpower to take it easy on you," he warns.

I start telling him to not take it easy on me when sits and he lowers me onto his cock, rapidly filling me. I gasp and grip his shoulders as he guides me to ride him. He lies back and drills into me, making me yell out. Elliot pulls me up when Daniel pauses, and slides into me.

"Oh fuck," I groan as they both start to slam into me.

"Lana," Daniel says. When she moves onto the bed, he grabs her and pulls her over top of him. He wraps his arms around her thighs, pulling her down to his mouth. She steadies herself with her hands on my shoulders but her eyes roll back immediately when he latches into her clit and sucks. He is still slamming into me while Elliot is tightly gripping my waist.

Lana keeps one hand on my shoulder to steady herself but brings the other down to tease my clit. It is almost instinctive that I respond by gently squeezing her breasts before pinching and teasing her nipples. As if we are on the same wavelength, we grab each other and press our lips together for a kiss. We keep one hand on each other to add to the pleasure that we are experiencing. We moan into each other as an orgasm hits us both.

We stay connected to each other, kissing. Elliott and Daniel are ruthless in the way they pull orgasms from us. I can't think straight when they overwhelm me like this. The added experience of Lana touching me is numbing my mind.

Daniel growls against Lana and she screams out her orgasm as he pushes into me and comes. With fluid movements, Elliot pulls me up so that Daniel can roll Lana to lie on the bed. She screams out again when he buries his face and continues to eat her. He pushes a few fingers into her and starts in on her hard and fast, with his hand.

Elliot pushes me down to lie across the bed before

slamming into me *"fuck,"* I scream.

"That's a good girl. Scream for me," Elliot commands. He braces his hands on either side of my body before starting to fuck me harder and harder. He doesn't let up and only drills into me deeper. My body aches and I scream through my orgasms. With one final thrust, Elliot pushes in deep as he comes.

They move me to the bed and I'm still violently shaking from the slew of orgasms. Elliot cleans me before we all lay in bed with Lana and me in the center facing each other. Elliot is behind me with his chest pressed against my back. Daniel is lying in the same way behind Lana and they both have their arms wrapped around us. I slip away into my dreams surrounded by comfort.

Chapter Twelve

Maya

I feel someone poking me in the forehead and I swat at them. "Go away," I complain.

"You need to wake up," Daniel says sweetly. I open my eyes and smile when I see him. He looks far more relaxed than he did last night when they first got to me. It makes me happy to see him happy.

"Why?" I ask.

"Because you told him you were going to do bloodwork," he says simply.

"I don't want to," I say.

"You don't have to, but why not?" he asks.

"I'm afraid he'll come after me again if he finds out I'm not biologically his," I say. "I can't keep doing this. I can't keep getting hurt by people."

"Do you want to know?" he asks, stroking my cheek.

"Yeah, I do. I want the truth but I know Mom will never give me the truth," I admit.

"Then let's go get this bloodwork done and we will take everything else day by day, yeah?"

"Yeah," I say with a smile. Daniel kisses the tips of my nose and I giggle at his playfulness. I get up and get dressed before going out to the living room.

Elliot and Lana smile when they see me. "Good

morning, sunshine," Lana says.

"Morning," I say, happily. "You guys could have woken me sooner, ya know?"

"You looked comfortable," Elliot says as he stands up from the couch to kiss me. "Did you sleep okay?"

"I did," I say.

"You were tossing and turning a lot, so I was hoping you weren't having a nightmare," he says.

"I hope I didn't keep you awake," I frown.

"I wasn't sleeping much anyway. You didn't keep me up."

"Feel free to kick me out of bed if I ever bother you doing that. The couch is comfortable anyhow," I say and he frowns at me.

"You're not sleeping on the couch," Elliot says firmly.

"See... Now you'll just wake up to me sleeping on the couch because I'll be restless and worried about keeping you up," I laugh. Elliot narrows his eyes and pulls me against his chest.

"If I wake up and catch you sleeping on the couch, you'll be punished," he says seriously.

"Oh no! Multiple orgasms... I'm so afraid," I say, faking a distressed voice before Lana and I break out into giggles.

"Try me and find out," he says, nearly growling. Fuck, that was hot. Being a brat to him is fun.

"Oh... I am *absolutely* going to try you," I say with a grin.

"Don't say I didn't warn you," he chuckles.

I glance at the couch and see that Daniel is spaced out, lost in thought. He looks genuinely upset. "What's wrong with Daniel?" I ask quietly

"Your guess is as good as mine," Lana says. "He's been like that since he woke up."

"He was fine when he came and woke me up," I frown.

"Don't think too much into it. He's the worst for bottling shit up," Elliot says. I shrug and walk over to the couch. It takes Daniel a moment to notice I'm in front of him.

"What's wrong?" I ask.

"Nothing," he says dismissively as he stands up. "Ready?"

"Mhmm," I say.

"What?" he sighs when I won't step out of his way.

"Nothing," I shrug and turn to the door. "I'm going to the car."

"Maya," he says, wanting me to stop and turn back to him.

"I'll meet you at the car," I say to Elliot, kissing him.

"Go easy on him," he says quietly.

"I don't like being lied to," I say simply before grabbing my bag and unlocking the front door. I pause for a second when I hear movement outside. I shake loose of that feeling, assuming I am overreacting, and open the door. I am immediately faced with Ivan, the driver, holding a box. I caught him right as he was about to knock on the door.

"Elliot," I nearly scream at him as I back up from Ivan. Daniel grabs me and pulls me away from the door as Elliot steps in front of me.

"Get the fuck off my property," Elliot growls.

"Don't worry," Ivan grins. "I'm just here to deliver something Ms. Sparks left behind." He hands Elliot what looks like the Kindle that they had in the bedroom. I pull away from Daniel and grab the Kindle. I already know this was Alexi's doing.

I open the front cover and there is a sticky note from Alexi on the screen.

Counting down until I feel your lips wrapped around my cock. -Alexi

Daniel and Lana read it over my shoulder. Daniel goes to grab it but rage fills me. I turn and step into the kitchen to get a screwdriver out of the junk drawer. They all watch me as I stab it through the screen before walking back over to them.

"Tell Alexi this is my response," I say to Ivan as I toss him the Kindle.

"You're playing a dangerous game, my dear," he chuckles. Ivan turns and walks off of the porch. We step out to see Alexi standing outside of the car with an amused look on his face. Ivan says something to Alexi when he reaches him as he hands him the Kindle. Alexi looks back at me and gives me that same annoying smile. It's a smile that tells me that he wants to turn me inside out for his pleasure.

We watch as they get back into the car and drive away. They are all watching me, waiting to see how I react. "Sick fucker," I snap, breaking the silence.

"Are you okay?" Elliot asks me, cupping my cheek.

"Yeah. I'm just angry," I say. "Let's go before I change my mind."

•••

We were silent for the entire drive to the lab. Elliot is the first to break the silence when he puts the car into park and turns to me. "Do you want us to all go in with you?"

"Please," I say quietly, staring at the building. Everyone gets out and Elliot opens my door and holds his hand out for me to take. When he stands me up from the car he pulls me close and hugs me.

"I love you, Maya," he says softly.

"I love you too," I say. I stay wrapped in his arms until Lana gets our attention.

"Uh… Guys… He's here," she says.

I look up to see Nikolai standing with someone I don't recognize by the front entrance, lost in conversation.

"I'm not worried about him," I say. "Not yet at least."

"Let's get this over with then," Elliot says with a smile as he puts his arm around my waist.

We all walk to the front entrance and Nikolai does a double-take when he sees me. "Maya," he says.

"I thought you said you'd handle Alexi?" I say, not caring who he's talking to.

"What happened?" he asks, frowning.

"He came to the house to bring me that Kindle and left a disgusting note about me blowing him," I say bluntly. Nikolai says something in Russian, no doubt cursing.

"He has clear instructions to stay away from you. I will talk to him," he says.

"Well, it was Ivan who came to the door. He said I was playing a dangerous game when I gave it back to him with a screwdriver through the screen."

"Okay, I will talk to Ivan as well. I apologize that they defied me," he says.

"Just keep to your word for once and get him to back the fuck off," I say. "How long until the results come back?"

"A few hours," Nikolai says.

"Alright," I say. "Good to know I have a few hours of freedom left." He sighs heavily but I walk away from him and walk inside before he can say anything.

"Name?" the woman says without looking up from her computer.

"Maya Sparks," I tell her as Nikolai walks in. She snaps her head up to look at me, then Nikolai.

"Give me just a second and we will get you back," she says hurriedly.

"Take your time," I say. We move to sit but a man comes out before we can.

"Ms. Sparks?" he says. I step to him and he waves me back with him. When the others walk with me he stops and glances at Nikolai.

"It's fine, Charlie. Let them come back with her," Nikolai says.

"Come on," he says to me with a smile.

I follow him back with Elliot, Daniel, and Lana behind me. He points for me to sit down before moving to gather what he needs.

"Ready?" he asks as he wipes my arm with an alcohol pad.

"Yep," I say curtly. He gives me a half smile before sticking me with the needle. I close my eyes and try not to think about the fact I may have been forced to blow my own father or that if he's not then he's my uncle and might kidnap me again. He'll likely force an abortion on me so he can get me pregnant with one that is biologically his. Do these people not understand what happens when you breed with your family? Incest can lead to deformities. Disgusting people.

When he wraps my arm and moves away from me, I open my eyes. "Nikolai said it won't take long?" I ask.

"No, just go get some lunch and I'll give you a call in an hour or two," he says.

"Thanks... I guess," I say. He nods and turns to his computer. When I step outside, Nikolai gives me a sympathetic smile.

"Thank you," Nikolai says.

"Try not to destroy the door again when you come after me," I say as I go to step past him. He grabs my arms and pulls me to a stop.

"What do I have to do to get you to understand that I'm not going to come after you?" he says as I jerk my arm out of his hold.

"Every time you have opened your mouth, you have lied to me," I say. "First you said it was Jonathan's debt. Then you said I had two months. Next, you told me it was actually one month or it doubled, but then you didn't actually give me two months. All to find out that it was Dad's debt and ten times less than I had to pay back. Which means you never planned on letting me pay. You had your men stalk me for a month and you fucking kidnapped me when you saw we had the money together. You forced me to get you off while I cried. You sat in that house and listened while your brother raped me. You expressed your plan to get me pregnant knowing that I was your niece at minimum. The second you think I am your biological daughter you want to play daddy and make up for what you did to me? What you let happen to me? Most uncles would kill for their nieces. Most families would do everything to protect each other, but you all just wanted to turn me into a toy. Isn't that what you kept calling me in Russian? You kept referring to me as your toy because I was yours to play with and yours to break," I say with a grave tone. "Now I fear that you'll kill my baby so you can force a baby made from rape and incest if I am just your niece. Incest, Nikolai. That's what all of this is. You consciously chose to try and fuck your niece so you could get her pregnant. Now you want me to trust your word?"

"Maya," he says in a tone like he's wanting me to calm down.

"Don't Maya me," I snap. "I was raped by my uncle. Now it's likely that I was forced to suck my father's dick minutes after he kidnapped me to avoid being gang raped by four people. That's what you did to me, Nikolai. Stop acting like it was a simple mistake. You sodomized your niece or your daughter then sent her off to be raped by her uncle. So to answer your question... short of killing yourself, there is nothing you can do to convince me that I have nothing to worry about. I will worry about me and my baby until the day you and Alexi die."

"I'm sorry, Maya," he says softly and I laugh.

"Fuck you, Nikolai," I say simply. "I hope I am your daughter so you can sit with all of that guilt that I see on your face right now. I hope it eats you alive."

I abruptly turn and walk to the car and wait for the others to catch up. I am raging on the inside with anger. Elliot senses that I don't want to be touched, so he and Lana simply get into the car. Daniel doesn't and reaches out for me but I stop him before he can hug me.

"What's wrong with you today?" I ask.

"Nothing," he says.

"Then keep your fucking hands off of me until you

can learn to stop lying to me," I say as I jerk the car door open. He grabs me and pushes me back against the car triggering Elliot to get out and watch us in fear of me spiraling.

"I am not lying to you, Maya. I am okay. I have a lot on my mind right now. When I am ready to talk about it, I will. Okay?" he says softly with his hands on my waist.

"Is it about me?" I ask. When he doesn't answer I shove him backward. I get in the car and the guys follow behind me.

"What do you want for lunch?" Elliot asks me.

"Just pick whatever. I'm not hungry," I say flatly as I stare out of my window.

"When did you eat last?" he asks.

"I'm not doing this with you right now, Elliot," I say.

"I know that you are angry right now, but I'm not asking you," he says. "You can be pissed off at me all you want, but you will eat lunch."

"Just pick something, Elliot. I don't care," I snap. I get my headphones out of my bag and put them in so I can listen to music and drown everything out for a minute. I'm getting angry at them when it's not their fault.

I know Daniel isn't intentionally leaving me out of his thoughts. It's obvious that something is going on that he is struggling with. Instead of just being patient, like he is with me, I was a bitch.

I know that Elliot is looking out for my well-being, but I was a bitch to him too. I need to take a moment to recenter my thoughts before I make it any worse. They don't deserve verbal abuse from me just because I'm in a bad mood.

Elliot lays his hand on my thigh as we drive and it instantly relaxes me. I put my hand on top of his as I lay my head back and close my eyes. I let the music carry me away to a place in my thoughts where I live a normal life free of trauma. I have normal parents who make corny jokes and support me unconditionally. My extended family is large and full of love and happiness. I don't have any trauma. I'm not afraid to be alone in the dark because I have never experienced waking up in a dark room to someone hitting me. I've never experienced being stolen from my home. No one has ever held me down and raped me while forcing me to come. This is part of my dreams, I am safe.

We get to a restaurant that Elliot has taken me to several times after I told him how much I enjoyed their food. I had a feeling that he would pick this place so I would be less likely to reject eating. I put my headphones away and sigh.

"I'm sorry for being a bitch," I say after a second.

"It's okay," Elliot says. "Believe it or not, we do know that you have emotions. We know that you only lash out at us because you feel safe enough to let those emotions out."

"I just... I am sick of being afraid. I'm sick of being lied to. I just want peace. That's all. I want one full day of peace every now and again. I want to just be with you all and not have a fear lurking in the back of my head that someone is going to hurt me," I say.

"One day at a time, remember?" Elliot says. "We will get there and I will make sure of it."

"Above all, I'm afraid of losing you guys. I can't picture my life without any of you and it scares me."

"We aren't going anywhere," Lana says. "I know it's hard to see that considering your past, but you are stuck with us."

"Well… I'll try to stop being shitty. I know you mean well and I know everyone has their own thing going on in their head," I say.

"Let's go eat," Elliot says before pulling me closer to kiss me.

We get out and go inside to eat lunch. Daniel is quiet and hardly looks at me the entire time. If I speak to him, he's short with me. It's giving me an overwhelming fear that I have seriously fucked up. Maybe it's about everything from last night. Maybe he's not down for the dynamic like he thought and he doesn't know how to tell me. Maybe I made him mad when I pushed him and he's just ignoring me for a while. I am sure I will figure it out eventually, but it doesn't stop me from worrying.

I order and eat an entire chicken caesar salad without issue. I have noticed that it's becoming easier to eat every day. Stress hinders that sometimes, but Elliot is incredibly helpful in those moments by simply not giving me a choice. It seems like a controlling move to make, but it's necessary. If allowed, I will go days without even thinking about food. I am seeing now how big of an issue that is.

My mood is finally starting to turn around until my phone starts to ring when we get into the car. "Go on. Answer it," Elliot says softly.

I sigh and answer it on speakerphone. "Hello?" I say.

"Is this Maya Sparks?" the man asks.

"It is."

"I am just calling with the results of the testing we did for you a few hours ago. Is now a good time?"

"It is," I say. "What are the results?"

"Nikoali Petrov is your biological father," he says simply.

"I assume he knows?" I ask.

"Yes. I just got off the phone with him," he says. "If you want a repeat test done, you can come by at any time. Nikolai also had me run bloodwork for your pregnancy in case you wanted to know your HCG levels or the gender."

"I assume he has those results too?" I ask with a sigh.

"No, ma'am. He instructed me to give you the results and destroy the record," the man says.

"Alright," I say. "What are the HCG levels?"

"8,547," he says. "I'd estimate that you are around six weeks pregnant. The date of conception was likely around three or four weeks ago."

"That tracks," I say before looking at Elliot. "Do you want to know?" I ask him.

"I do," he nods.

"What's the gender?" I ask.

"You're having a girl," he says. Elliot smiles brightly which triggers my own grin.

"He told you to tell me after the results, didn't he?" I ask.

"He did," he says.

"Well... Thank you for calling," I say.

"Have a wonderful day, Ms. Sparks," he says before hanging up. Elliot grabs my face and kisses me. When he pulls away he is still smiling.

"Are you excited?" I ask.

"More than I think you realize," he says. "Let's go home. I need to get some work done so I don't get behind on paperwork."

"You mean we? Didn't you hire me to help you with that stuff?" I ask.

"Okay," he laughs. "We. You can come sit on my lap

and help."

"Why do I feel like we aren't going to be getting much work done?"

"We'll get some work done so long as you sit still," he laughs.

Chapter Thirteen

Maya

When we get home, Daniel disappears into his and Lana's room while she sits down to watch TV. I change into more comfortable clothes before joining Elliot in his office.

"Hey," I say as I lean down to kiss Elliot. I squeal when he suddenly grabs me and pulls me into his lap.

"I have to be on a video conference in a second. I completely forgot about it," he says.

"So I probably shouldn't be in your lap," I laugh.

"Probably not, but you can certainly stay close by," he says as he loads up the video conference.

"How long will the meeting take?" I ask.

"About a half hour. It's just the monthly recap with all of my managers," he says.

"That reminds me," I say. "We should go by the bar so I can tell Fiona in person about me being pregnant."

"She will love that," he laughs.

"I feel bad that I haven't hung out with her much. I just didn't want Nikolai to latch onto her," I say.

"She understands. Maybe now things can calm down," he says as the video loads. "Okay. It won't be long and you can come back and sit with me."

I get off his lap and move to sit on the desk beside his laptop. An idea comes to mind as soon as he greets everyone. I grin at him and he smirks, trying to pay attention. When I get up he doesn't pay much attention, but when I sink to my knees, he holds his hand up to tell me no. I ignore him and quietly unbutton his jeans so I can pull him out. He moves his chair back a few inches to make room for me.

I have never done this with him, but I think it's because he's afraid it will trigger me. This means he doesn't know that I can take all of him without issue. I immediately take him down my throat and he unexpectedly groans.

"Everything okay?" A man asks.

"Yeah. Uh. Sorry. Keep going," Elliot manages as I slowly suck his cock. I am going to intentionally draw it out as much as I can. I give him just enough to keep him on the edge. He has a tight grip on my hair but doesn't take control. I want him to though. I want him to grab my face and fuck my throat. I want him to use me for his pleasure. I will break him one day and get him to face fuck me!

He clicks a button on his laptop to mute himself before glancing down at me. "Jesus Christ, Maya," he says. He has his elbow on the desk as he casually puts his hand over his mouth. He is sitting back and from the camera's perspective, he looks completely relaxed.

He looks down at me again and I take the opportunity to see his reaction. I gently cup his balls and his eyes roll back for a moment and he tightens his grip on my hair when I gently squeeze as I take him all of the way down my throat. He's not fucking my throat but he also doesn't let me pull away now. When I try he growls at me, knowing it's only to talk shit before sucking him down again.

I maintain this torture of edging him throughout the entire meeting. If he had just forced himself down my throat like I was trying to get him to do, I would have let him come thirty minutes ago. Instead, I am drawing it out for fun.

When he shuts his laptop after the meeting I cup him and squeeze a bit harder and I get a moan out of him. He has both hands on my head this time as he keeps eye contact with me. I can see it on his face that he wants to do it, but won't. I try one last thing before I let him win and slow down significantly. I stop sucking and simply have him in my mouth.

"Fuck, Maya," he groans. I hum in response to my name and it nearly breaks him. I can feel the tension in how he's holding me. There is no way I'm getting away from this man before he comes. I take him all the way down before humming again, and I can feel that he's about to break. I hum once more as I squeeze him harder, this time it forces a deep guttural groan from him. With that, he breaks.

Elliot stands with my lips still wrapped around his cock before holding the sides of my face. When he starts to fuck my throat, he starts slowly. The more he forces on me, the harder I suck him. I have my hands on his thighs when it all clicks for him and he sets in on ravaging my throat.

"Oh fuck, that's good," he moans. "Is this what you want, Maya? You want me to treat you like my whore?" I hum in response and he fully lets go and fucks my throat hard and fast. My body is pulsating with need as he takes what he wants. His moans are becoming labored and his pace waivers as he pushes himself as far down my throat as he can.

"Fuck. Swallow, Maya. Take every fucking drop," he growls as he unloads himself. I greedily suck him, swallowing everything he has gifted me. When he pulls out of my mouth, he sits back down and fixes his pants.

I sit back on my heels and wipe the drool from my chin. "You're an evil woman, Maya," he says breathlessly.

"You could have made me take you at any moment," I remind him. "You tortured yourself."

"I hear you," he smirks. When I stand up he grabs me and pulls me into his lap to straddle him. "You seem tense."

"Ah. Yeah. I just kind of tortured myself too," I say with a sweet smile.

"Does it turn you on when I fuck your throat like that?" he asks and I nod, still smiling. "You know I will find a way to repay you for torturing me, right?"

"I'm hoping so," I say simply.

"Do I want to know how in the hell you're so good at that?" he asks.

"Probably not," I smile. "But... you get all of the benefits from it."

There is a knock at the door before Lana comes in. "Hey," she says.

"Hi," I smile.

"So... I think I know what's going on with Daniel. I wanted to tell you two before he inevitably comes clean," she says as she sits on the desk and I turn to face her.

"What's up?" Elliot asks.

"I think that he is realizing his feelings for Maya and it's scaring him," she says.

"Yeah. That would do it," Elliot says.

"Meaning?" I ask.

"I think Daniel realized last night that he loves you

as more than just a friend. I know that I am his priority but I think he's afraid of offending Elliot or scaring you."

"What can I do?" I ask.

"Keep bugging the shit out of him. Be a brat. Tease him. You'll find the right button and he will let it out. Once he does, he will relax," she explains.

"Is he still hiding?" I ask.

"No. I got him to come to the living room," she says.

"Gonna go torture him next?" Elliot asks.

"You complain but we both know you loved it," I say before kissing him and getting out of his lap. "I'm just going to be annoying."

"For peace of mind," Lana says. "What are your feelings about Daniel?"

"I am not in love with him like I am Elliot or he is with you, but I do love him. I love his presence. I love how well he treats me. I love how kind he is and how happy he makes me. I don't think I could picture my life without him in it as more than just my friend. I want to marry Elliot one day but that doesn't change the fact that I want to be committed to both of them and you. You all make me happy and I feel like I make you guys happy so I want us to all stay together."

"You want to marry me?" Elliot asks with a smile.

"Well, we both agreed that we wanted a baby, so I figured that that was a given," I laugh.

"Don't tell him any of that until you make him open up first," Lana says. "Also, you guys should just go to one of the wedding chapels and get married. Get rid of that fucking last name."

"I mean..." I say as Elliot stands up and cups my face.

"Really think about what you are going to say

because I will take you today and marry you," Elliot says seriously.

"Maya Greene has a nice ring to it," I say with a sweet smile.

"Yay!" Lana says as she hugs us. "Go annoy Daniel. Maybe tease him until he bends you over."

"Oh, I'm sold," I laugh.

"What did you do to Elliot?" Lana asks as we leave the office.

"Gave him head while he was on his video call meeting," I laugh. "Even after, I kept edging him until he went all feral on me."

"Oh, that's hot. Definitely go tease Daniel," she laughs. "He won't go as hard on you as he does me though. When I tease him he bruises my cervix."

"That sounds painful but amazing," I laugh.

Daniel glances up from the TV when we get to the living room but avoids looking at me. I stand by the couch with my hands on my hips staring at him, waiting for him to look at me.

"What, Maya?" he asks with a sigh when he finally looks at me.

"You will hardly look at me and it's hard to not be offended by that," I say honestly. Instead of saying something, he ignores me and picks up the remote. I stepped forward, snatch it out of his hand, and toss it to the other side of the couch. "Are you mad at me?"

"What? No, Maya. Why would I be mad at you?" he asks.

"Then can I sit with you and you try to stop acting like you're mad?"

"Yeah," he says. "Come sit with me."

I know he expects me to sit beside him, so it takes

him by surprise when I climb into his lap to straddle him. "Maya," he sighs.

"Nope. You are done moping. Whatever is going on, we are figuring it out right now," I say.

"I'm not in the right headspace for this, Maya," he says.

"I don't care," I shrug. "What's going on?"

"It's not a big deal, Maya," he says dismissively.

"This is the first time I have sat in your lap and you have not put your hands on me. You are lying to me again," I say simply and he sighs.

"Unless of course, all of this is because you are not attracted to me and don't know how to tell me," I challenge him.

"You know that's not true," he frowns.

"I don't know that. You were fine when it was just you and me this morning when you woke me up. The second you are around Elliot or Lana, you start acting like you don't want me around. So it's either you don't find me attractive or you just simply don't wanna be around me anymore."

"Maya. Stop it. You know that's not true," he says firmly.

"I mean. I wouldn't blame you if you weren't attracted to me anymore," I say.

"Maya," he growls.

"I'm honestly surprised you were even able to be with me before. If that's the case, you can just tell me. I'm used to hearing it so it's not gonna upset me or anything," I say. Daniel literally growls before grabbing my face and pulling me closer to where we are almost nose to nose.

"I know what you are doing and being a brat is not going to get me to tell you," Daniel says.

"Is it just my face in general or is it size related?" I ask.

"Stop," he says in a grave tone.

"Probably size. Not everyone is into fat girls," I say, with a sweet smile. I glance up at Elliot and Lana and they both look highly amused. "I can do this all night, Daniel."

"You are starting to piss me off, Maya," he says as he grips my waist tightly.

"Ahh. So it is my face then?" I mean, I don't blame you there either. But hey... At least we know that you can still get hard for me," I say as I roll my hips against him. He groans and presses his erection against my center. "Tell me, Daniel."

"Not right now," he says as his hands fall away from me.

"Tell me," I say again. "I don't like feeling like you don't wanna be around me anymore. You won't look at me, you won't touch me, and you probably don't even want me sexually. This is simply just a reaction to someone sitting in your lap."

"Maya. You are pushing me," he warns.

"I'm not stopping until you tell me," I say.

"Good luck," he says.

"Tell me... how were you able to get hard from me before? Right now I understand, since I'm on top of you. Maybe you just thought you were into chubby girls," I say. "Like a fat lover phase or something."

"Say it one more time," Daniel warns.

"What? Fat lover phase or you thought you were into chubby girls?" I ask. I squeal when he suddenly flips us where I am pinned on the couch with him straddling me. He has my arms pulled above my head so that I can't move. "Tell me, Daniel. Please."

"I love you, Maya. More than I feel like I should and it scares me. I don't want to fuck up anything with Lana. I don't want to fuck up anything with Elliot. But I can't stand not being around you. Lana is the love of my life, but you are so fucking special to me. I would choose Lana over and over again, but that doesn't mean I wouldn't be any less miserable without you," he explains.

"I love you too, Daniel," I say as I lean up and kiss him softly. "I will always choose Elliot as well, but I want you to be a part of my life, long-term. I want all of you to be a part of my life long-term."

"If you felt that way, why didn't you say something?" he asks.

"Why didn't you?" I counter.

"Good point," he says with a smile. "If you ever call yourself fat again, I'll fuck you to tears. Understand?"

"You know..."

"Maya. Don't," he warns, making Lana and Elliot laugh.

"Before he destroys you, you should tell him," Elliot says.

"Oh! Elliot and I are going to get married," I say happily.

"When?" Daniel asks.

"When you get done with her," Elliot says. "She's on something today with the teasing."

"Is that right?" Daniel asks me.

"Yeah. I blew him while he was in a video conference and edged him the entire time. I wanted to break him so that he would face fuck me," I giggle.

"And now you want to get fucked after turning yourself on?"

"Mhmm," I smile. "So I'm definitely going to keep

saying degrading things about myself until you do. Have I mentioned how unattractive you guys should find me?"

Daniel sits back on his heels and pulls my shorts and underwear off before flipping me to my belly. "Don't say I didn't warn you to stop," he says as thrusts deep inside of me. His pace is immediately unrelenting and has me yelling out in comprehendible words as he fucks me hard and fast.

"Fuck fuck fuck," I yell.

Just as my orgasm is about to peak, he stops and pulls out of me. I whine in protest and Daniel chuckles as he kisses my cheek.

"You're ours to take, pretty girl," he says as he slides into my ass with force. I gasp and grip the couch cushion as he stretches me. He offers me no time to adapt to his size before he starts, pounding me into the couch. There's a beautiful mixture of pain and pleasure floating through my body as he punishes me for degrading myself. My moans get caught in my throat and my orgasm slowly and silently moves through me, making my body tense. Deep groans start to come out of me when he moans my name in my ear. He pushes into me deeper, making me gasp, as he comes deep inside of me.

"Dear God, Daniel," I groan as he pulls out of me and fixes my shorts.

"The next time you say something bad about yourself, I'll make sure you have tears running down that pretty little face of yours when I'm done with you," he says as he leans down to whisper in my ear.

"Where the fuck did that come from," I ask as he pulls me up to sit.

"You didn't sound like you were complaining to me," Daniel says with a smirk.

"No, not at all," I laugh breathlessly.

"Are you two really getting married today?" he asks.

"Yeah. We chose to try and get pregnant, we may as well get married too," I say. "Do you and Lana want to come with us?"

"Yes!" Lana says happily.

"Go get cleaned up and we can go," Elliot says as he leans over the back of the couch to kiss me.

I hop up and go to the bedroom. Once I am clean, I change into a pink floral wrap dress and slip on sandals. I let my hair down before walking out to the living room.

"You look hot," Lana says.

"Thanks," I laugh. "Ready?"

"Yes Ma'am," Elliot says before kissing me. "Let's get married

Chapter Fourteen

Maya

Elliot puts the car in park before we all get out. "I'm excited," I say happily as Elliot takes me by the hand.

"Me too," he smiles. "You sure you want to marry me?"

"Very sure!"

"You two are just the cutest," Lana says as we walk inside.

Elliot and I fill out the necessary paperwork before choosing our package. We decided on the most basic because we do not need anything over the top to prove that we want to be together. I have never been so sure of something in my life before. Maybe we are rushing things, but after the life I have lived I think acting on what makes me happy is acceptable.

Part of me wishes my Mom were here. Maybe that comes from the part of my brain that there is still that little girl holding out hope that she cares. If she did, she wouldn't have left me here where she undoubtedly knew Nikolai would get to me. She knew that he would want revenge. She sacrificed her only daughter to move across the country, to safety. I have a good mind to fly to Florida and go see her and demand answers. Maybe completely cutting ties with her after saying my piece is what I need to officially move on from the idea that she was an actual mother to me. Her version of protection was to send me out of the house for hours at a time without checking in on my well-being. She never once checked in on me to make sure the neighbors weren't hurting me. She never made sure no one kidnapped me. Anything could have happened and she wouldn't have known until it was too late.

Elliot and I go through our little ceremony with Daniel and Lana beside us. We are both nearly bursting with excitement as we repeat back the vows to the officiant. When he pronounces us husband and wife, we kiss each other like no one else is in the room. At that moment, the only things that matter are each other.

When we finally pull away from one another, Lana grabs my face and kisses me hard. The officiant is slightly taken aback by her approach, but that is Lana for you. "Congratulations, Maya," she says with a sweet smile.

"Thank you for coming with us," I say as I hug her.

Daniel picks me up in a hug and spins me around before kissing me. "Lana and I have to give you two a wedding present later," he says, winking. Elliot softly kisses Lana after hugging her.

"I hope my part of the gift is to watch," Elliot says, chuckling.

"Oh, it is," Lana laughs.

"Thank you so much," I say to the officiant, who looks rightfully shaken. For being Vegas, he sure does look shocked by our dynamic.

We all go back to the parking lot and Elliot hugs me tightly. "I love you so much, Maya," he says softly.

"I love you too, Elliot," I reply happily. "Can we go grab dinner somewhere?" Elliot pulls away and everyone gives me a strange look. "What?"

"I've just never heard you ask that before," Elliot says. "Where do you want to go?"

"I really want Birria tacos," I say.

"That is how you combat an eating disorder with Maya apparently," Lana says. "Just knock her up and those cravings will handle the rest."

I laugh and shake my head at her. "I was thinking about them all the way here."

"Let's go get some tacos then," Elliot chuckles. We get into the car and Elliot finds a restaurant that serves Birria tacos.

Birra is a meat stew. I always have it with beef, but some people use a variety of other meats. The beef is marinated in an adobo made of vinegar, onion, guajillo chiles, ancho chiles, arbol chiles, garlic, cumin, ground clove, oregano, cinnamon stick, black peppercorns, and bay leaves. It can be served as a stew, or you can dip tortillas in the consomé, then fry it in a hot skillet. You then top it with Cilantro, onion, and lime juice then enjoy. It is absolutely mouthwatering. It's one of the few things I will easily push through my fear of foods to eat.

We get to the restaurant and order. I am lost in thought, wanting to confront my Mom. Lana notices how quiet I am first.

"What's wrong?" she asks.

"Oh, nothing," I say. "I'm just thinking."

"About?" Elliot asks, eating a tortilla chip.

"Would you all come with me if I went to Florida?" I ask.

"Of course," Elliot says. "Wanting to see your Mother?"

"Yeah. I just want to try to get answers so I can say my piece and officially cut ties with her. I want her to know where I stand. Maybe I should just go on with my life, but I just want to get it out there, ya know? I figured it would be better to do it now before I get too pregnant. Plus, it will get me away from Nikolai and Alexi for a while."

"When do you want to go? We can all work remotely," Elliot asks.

"Uh... The sooner the better. I'd rather not be stuck on a plane if morning sickness hits me. I'd like to get there and come home as soon as possible," I say.

"Oh, that's a good point," Lana says. "That might hit you any day now."

"Let's look at flights then," Elliot says as he pulls out his phone.

"Do you two want to come with us?" I ask Lana.

"Duh," Lana says, giving me a weird look.

"Sorry," I laugh. "I don't know how these things work."

"We are a team, Maya," Daniel says. "Just because Lana and I are married and you and Elliot are married doesn't mean we aren't all committed to one another individually and as a group."

"I don't even know what to call us, individually or as a group," I laugh.

"Well, I'm your wife now," Lana says with a grin as she sips her margarita.

"Does that make Daniel her second husband?" Elliot asks, laughing.

"That would make Lana your second wife," I add.

"Wait," Lana says. "Daniel and Elliot can be husbands then."

"Hey, there ya go," I laugh.

"You two are silly," Elliot says. "There is a

flight leaving tomorrow afternoon to Palm Beach International."

"That works. How much are the tickets?" I ask. "We'll need to get a hotel or something."

"We can just rent a beach house," Elliot says as he types on his phone.

"How much are the tickets?" I ask again.

"Why?" he asks.

"So I can pay for mine. Is it a secret?" I ask.

"Baby, we are married. My money is your money," he says, not looking up from his phone.

"Oh," I say.

"It's just something to get used to," he says.

"Yeah. Clearly, I'm only just now learning what healthy relationships should look like," I laugh.

When our food gets to the table, I eat and listen to the others talk about different things we can do in Florida while we are there to turn it into a mini honeymoon. I feel as though they are worried things will go bad so they want to fill our time with activities to help keep my mind off of the negativity. They have come to learn my anxiety well and have figured out ways to help me not fall so hard when something triggers me or my PTSD.

Elliot finishes booking the flight and the beach house before setting his phone down and eating the rest of his dinner. I am, surprisingly, the first one done. They all make a point to not bring attention to me when I eat without issues. The few times they have, I have ended up regressing and struggling for a few days. It seems almost childish that I struggle so much with eating, but they all constantly reassure me that it is not childish and it is mental health. They are huge advocates for my mental health and have taught me so much about myself through my journey with prioritizing my mental health.

"I'm going to go to the bathroom before we leave," I say as I get up from the booth. I ate entirely too fast because now I am nauseous. Although, that could be pregnancy-related also.

When I get done in the bathroom, I go to the sink to wash my hands. I get my phone out to look at the flight confirmation that Elliot just texted me as I go to the door. When I open it I look up when I sense I am about to run into someone.

My heart nearly leaps out of my chest and I instinctively back up when I find myself face-to-face with Alexi and Ivan. He has that stupid smirk on his face as they step in.

"You need to go," I say with a shaky voice.

"Is that right?" he asks as he flips the lock and leaves Ivan at the door to walk closer to me.

"Nikolai told you to stay away from me," I say. I search the room for anything to use against him. I am locked in here with him and there is no way I am getting past Ivan.

"I don't answer to Nikolai," he laughs. "Why do you look so scared, Maya? Can't I just have a nice conversation with my niece?"

"You're fucking sick," I snap at him.

"I am about sick of your attitude," he says, stepping closer to me.

"Fuck you," I say with my voice breaking.

"You're my pet now, puppet," he says with a malicious grin. Before I can react he grabs me by the hair and shoves me toward the sink. He covers my mouth before I can scream out so all of my noises are muffled. Ivan approaches and slaps duct tape over my mouth as

Alexi pulls the tie on my dress and yanks it off of me.

Alexi rips my underwear off before lifting me to lay me across the counter with my face pushed against the mirror. I scream against the tape on my mouth when he bites down on my ass. "Such a grade-A piece of meat. Nikolai was foolish for letting you go," Alexi says.

"He's my father, you sick fuck," I scream at him through my tape.

"Matter's not, you're good breeding stock and we are not as closely related as you believe," Alexi says casually as he spreads my ass and spits on me. I start screaming as he pulls his dick and presses it against my tight hole. "But this... Right here... Is to remind you of your place, Puppet."

Alexi rams himself into my ass with so much force that my screams break and I can feel him tear me with his size. He brutally and forcibly fucks me into the mirror while I scream in pain. His hands are gripping my hips so tightly that I know I'll have bruises by the time he's done with me. The pain stabs through my abdomen with every thrust he makes into my body. The room is filled with the sounds of my muffled screams and his skin vigorously slapping against mine. Everything is blurry from my tears blinding me.

Alexi's movements are rapid and punishing. The first time he wanted to degrade me by making me come, but this time the metallic smell in the air solidifies his desire to make me bleed; a reminder of his power over me.

With one final and violent surge, he groans as he comes inside me. When he pulls out and tucks himself away, he steps back to let me fall from the counter to a heap on the white tile floor. I quickly grab my dress to cover myself before backing myself into the corner between the wall and the sink.

Alexi leans down and rips the duct tape off of my mouth, making my sobs vocal again. "I'll be seeing you again soon, Puppet," Alexi says with a feigned cheerfulness in his voice. "Remember your place."

He stands up and straightens his suit jacket before walking out of the bathroom with Ivan. My sobs turn hysterical when the door shuts and I am alone. The emotional anguish running through my mind is overwhelming and consumes everything inside of me. I bring myself down to lie on the floor, tightly gripping the dress around me as I cry. I can't differentiate between reality and the agony I feel, both mentally and physically. I know that I am hurt because the pain is still surging through my backside. The silver lining to the pain is it's a constant reminder that I am alive. I am in pain, so I survived.

I don't hear the door open over my hysterical sobs as I am curled up in the fetal position on the cold floor. "Oh my God, Maya," I hear Lana scream as she rushes to my side. She kneels on the floor and pulls me up enough to wrap her arms around me. She is holding me so tight that it aches, but it's comforting.

"It was Alexi," I manage to force out through my sobs.

"I'm so sorry, Maya. I should have come with you. I'm so sorry," she says as she gently rocks me.

"What happened?" Elliot asks as the bathroom door is slung open. "Oh God, Maya."

"It was Alexi," Lana says as Elliot pulls me from her. He cups my face to get me to look at him.

"What happened, Maya? Where is the blood coming from? What did he do?" Elliot asks.

"He raped me," I whimper.

"That's a lot of blood, Elliot," Lana says softly.

"Fuck. I know," Elliot sighs heavily as he hugs me.

"I'll go talk to the manager," Lana says. "Daniel, go get the car so we can take her to the hospital."

Elliot lets go of me so Daniel can lean down and hug me. "I'm going to fucking kill him for this," Daniel says, hardly containing his anger. He kisses my head before leaving to get the car.

Elliot holds me until Lana can get back. The manager is with her and gasps when she sees me.

"We need to call the cops," she says.

"No," I say. "No, it'll just have them come after this place."

"It's the mafia," Lana says. "Just clean the place up. We are going to take her to the hospital. I just wanted you to see it so no customers did."

"Shit. Okay. We've had some run-ins with them. Go get her checked out," she says. "Take her out of the back so she doesn't have people staring at her."

"I'll text Daniel and tell him where to take the car," Lana says as she pulls out her phone. Elliot helps me stand up so he can put my dress back on me before scooping me up in his arms. I turn into his chest as he carries me out of the restaurant. When he gets me into the back seat, he sits with me while Lana sits in the front with Daniel.

I am lying with my head in Elliot's lap as he gently strokes my head. When he gets his phone out, I know who he is going to call.

"What's wrong?" Nikolai says when he answers.

"You gave Maya your word that you'd handle Alexi. You want to make amends and yet you can't even keep her safe?" Elliot growls.

"What happened, Elliot? Is Maya okay?"

"No, she's not okay, Nikolai," Elliot snaps. "Alexi cornered her in a goddamn bathroom and raped her again. Now she's bleeding and we have to take her to the hospital."

"You can't take her to the hospital, Elliot. They'll want to do a rape kit," he says.

"Maybe she should. Maybe it's time we brought the police into this."

"He will kill her, Elliot. If she goes to the cops, she'll be dead by morning. You can't take her anywhere near that place or the cops," Nikolai pleads. He sounds genuinely worried for me right now, which is admittedly nice.

"She is pregnant with our daughter and bleeding and you want me to just not fucking take her? Are you fucking stupid, Nikolai?"

"Elliot. I will bring an OB to have her checked. They will do an ultrasound and make sure everything is okay. How did he rape her? Maybe it's not pregnancy-related," he says.

"I don't know.." he starts to say.

"Anally," I whisper. Elliot sighs before continuing.

"He raped her anally," Elliot says. "I still want her checked."

"Of course. Take her home and I'll be there soon. Does anyone else know?"

"Just the manager of La Amigos. We told her not to call the cops. She's going to clean up so no one else sees," Elliot explains.

"Was anyone with him?"

"Ivan," I say.

"Fuck. Okay. We will talk more when I get there.

I'm going to bring someone I trust to do a sweep and make sure Alexi isn't tracking you all in any way. He has a history of bugging people he sees as targets to keep track of them," Nikolai says. "Don't make any calls or texts from Maya's phone until it can be checked. I don't trust that he's not watching her."

"Fine," Elliot says.

"Thank you, Nikolai," I say. He's a psycho and definitely doesn't have to help me, so I'll give him credit where credit is due.

"You're welcome, Maya. Go home and shower if you want. Just relax, okay?" Nikolai says.

"Okay," I sigh.

"We'll see ya," Elliot says as he hangs up.

We ride in silence to the house and Elliot strokes my head the whole way. Daniel and Lana look back every now and again to check on me. I know I should be more distraught over this. Maybe I should be having a meltdown right now. All I want to do is take a shower and go to sleep surrounded by Elliot, Lana, and Daniel. I feel safe when I am snuggled up in bed with them.

When we get home I am in far less pain than I was and I don't think I'm bleeding anymore. I still want to make sure the baby is okay. I've always been easy to bleed when I would be injured in some way, so it's likely not as bad as it seems. I would be in a lot more pain if I was.

Elliot walks with me up the porch stairs as Daniel insists on going first to check the house. When he comes back to the door, Elliot scoops me up and brings me inside. I smile at this, even though I know it's because he wants to take me to bed and not because I'm his bride now.

"What?" Elliot asks with a soft smile to match

mine.

"You carried me in like I'm your bride," I say.

"Because you are my bride," he says. "So you want to shower?"

"Yeah. Can you come with me? I don't want to be alone," I say.

"Yeah. Of course," he says. "Daniel, if they get here while she's in the shower just let them know we will be out in a bit."

"No problem. Take your time," Daniel says. He kisses me softly before Lana comes over and kisses me as well.

Elliot takes me to the bathroom and sets me on my feet before starting the shower. When I take my dress off I see the fingerprint bruising forming on my hips and frown. "Christ almighty," Elliot says.

"Yeah," I say flatly.

"What's the bruise on your butt from?" He questions as he helps me take my bra off.

"The psycho bit me. Is it bad?" I ask.

"Uh. Yeah. He didn't break skin though. Who the fuck bites someone?"

"Alexi, apparently. I knew he was going to bruise my hips. He was so fucking violent about everything," I say. Elliot steps me into the shower and immediately sets in on washing my body.

"What happened?" he asks. "You don't have to tell me though. I just want you to be able to if you want."

"No, it's okay. I want to say it," I say. I go over every gruesome detail of the situation. He washes my body thoroughly as I talk.

"I knew I should have walked with you. The bathroom was so far away from everyone... We didn't hear anything until Lana screamed when she went in. Lana was going to check on you because she thought you got sick."

"That place was loud with the music," I say. "Shit happens. This isn't on you, baby. He made it very clear to me that he can get to me anywhere. Know my place, remember?"

"Your place is beside me, not under that fucking psycho," Elliot snaps. "I'm sorry... I fucking hate that I feel like I can't protect you. I can't go to the cops. I can't take you to the damn hospital. I can't do anything because it's the fucking mafia. Luckily Jonathan is minding his own business and we aren't having to worry about him too. I just want to make this better but I can't. That fucking rat bastard is making it impossible."

"Since when am I the calm one!" I ask with a smile and he relaxes when he chuckles.

"We'll get through this," Elliot says as he kisses me.

"I know," I say as he rinses the conditioner out of my hair.

"Can we still go to Florida?" I ask.

"Of course we can. Going across the country for a week sounds like a wonderful idea," he says as he washes himself. "You aren't bleeding anymore?"

"No. I think it was just from how he raped me, honestly. I always bleed easier with being iron deficient," I say.

"Seeing that blood scared me," he admits. "It wasn't a lot, but it was enough."

"Yeah. I'm okay though," I say as Elliot shuts the water off. He wraps me in a towel before helping me out of the shower. "You're going to baby me, aren't you?"

"My pregnant wife just got assaulted again. The

least I could do is wait on her hand and foot," he says with a smile. "I like taking care of you."

"It is nice," I admit. I get dressed in shorts and one of Elliot's T-shirts before he brushes and dries my hair.

When we get out to the living room Nikolai and two random people are sitting with Lana and Daniel. Daniel jumps up and comes over to hug me. "You're just as bad as Elliot with worrying. I'm okay," I say.

"Wish you'd stop saying that," he says with a frown.

"I'm alive. I'm okay, Daniel," I say and he kisses me.

"You're going to freak out Nikolai like you all did the officiant," I laugh. I turn to Nikolai who is standing and watching me carefully. I know he's going to do it before he approaches me so it doesn't catch me off guard when he hugs me.

"Well this is weird," Lana says when I hug him back. I don't know why but I feel like I at least owe him this if he is making an effort to help me. He doesn't have to. It doesn't mean I hate him any less, but I can be the bigger person.

"I know you hate me and I know there is no way for me to redeem myself, but you're just going to have to deal with me worrying about you for a while," he says when he pulls away.

"I still hope you die painfully and alone," I say with a smile and he laughs.

"I'm sure I will. At this rate, it'll probably be Alexi who does it. I've done everything short of killing this man and he apparently won't listen. Going after you again means he needs to be taken care of for good."

"Well, I don't disagree," I say.

"This is Dr. Olagard. She is an OB. That is Joshua. He

is a computer engineer who does work for me. He's going to do a sweep of the house if anyone wants to follow him."

"I did find a tracker on the silver car outside," Joshua says. "It's been destroyed now."

"Ah. Great," I say.

"Is this easier with her in the bedroom?" Elliot asks the doctor.

"Yes. It'll also be more private," she says.

Daniel kisses me again before going off with Joshua. Elliot and Lana have me go back to the bedroom and lie down. Nikolai stays in the hallway.

"I'd like to check your cervix if that's okay," she says. "Nikolai says the rape was not vaginal, right?"

"Yeah," I say quietly.

"Okay. Like I told him, everything is more than likely fine, but I will check as if I didn't know any of that. I'd rather be safe than sorry and something actually be wrong. Just slip your shorts off when you are ready and I'll walk you through everything as I do it," she says and Lana hands me a throw blanket so I don't have to be fully exposed.

I take a deep breath and take my shorts off while the doctor turns her attention to her bag to set up what she needs. Once I am covered up and she is ready she turns back to me.

"Okay, so just bring your feet together and let your knees fall apart. I'm just going to use the speculum to see your cervix and I'll be done with that part," she says. I do as she asks and drape my arm over my face. Elliot is sitting beside me and leans down on his elbow so he can move my arm and look at me. He doesn't say anything but he cups my face and strokes my cheek with his thumb.

Lana is watching the doctor. I'm surprised she's not

asking more questions or anything. She's becoming just as protective as Elliot and Daniel.

"Okay. So your cervix looks great. We will take a look at the baby in a second but I'd like to see how severe the damage is from the rape itself," she says.

"Okay," I say with a small voice.

"It's going to be easier if you roll to your belly," she says softly.

"Fuck," I sigh.

"We are right here," Elliot says. I nod and roll to my stomach.

The doctor had Lana help so that the process goes quicker. The moment she puts her hands on me I start crying again. Elliot rubs my back to soothe me while she does what she needs to do. When she's done, Lana helps me back into my shorts and I lie back on my back.

"The tearing is minimal. You'll be sore for a few days, but it should heal fine. How's the pain?"

"It's gone away now," I say.

"Good, okay. Do you have any questions?" she asks.

"What about anal sex?" Lana asks.

"Lana," I say, laughing.

"What? You are more or less married to two men and a woman. It's good to know," she says with a shrug and the doctor chuckles.

"I'd say give it a few days at minimum. When you do, use lots and lots of lube. More than you think you need. That will ensure you don't redamage yourself," she says. "You're pretty early still, but we should be able to see the heartbeat." She gets out a portable ultrasound and sets it up. She puts jelly in my lower abdomen and presses a wand to me, pushing in slightly. I get a wave of anxiety, because what if something is wrong?

"Everything okay?" Lana asks after a second.

"Yeah. I just normally have techs do this," she laughs. "Ah. Here we go." She turns the screen to us and I see a little bean shaped blob with a tiny flicker of light in its middle.

"She's okay?" I ask.

"She's perfect," Dr. Olagard says with a smile. She hits a button and the baby's rapid thumping heartbeat fills the room making me relax instantly. When I look at Elliot, who is gripping my hand tightly, he has tears in his eyes and he is smiling. He leans down and kisses me. "Babies, especially at this stage, are very well protected. Nikolai explained a little of what is going on. What I will tell you is that if this becomes a habit of Alexi's then you are okay as long as no foreign objects are introduced, outside of normal toys. At that point, I would be concerned for damage, especially if it's anything sharp. Do your best to avoid that and the baby will be fine. That might change as you get further along, but we can address that if we come to it."

"Thank you," I say.

"You're welcome," she says as she hands me a card. "This is my office. I'd love to get you set up there so I can keep following your care. Nikolai gave me very strict instructions that no one is to know that you are pregnant, so seeing me will ensure that we can keep this under wraps for as long as possible."

I get up from the bed while she packs up her stuff and I go to the hallway to update Nikolai. When I open the door, Nikolai is standing with Daniel and Joshua. "Hey," I say.

"Everything okay?" Daniel asks as he hugs me.

"Yeah. I'm okay, Daniel," I say softly. "Damage is

minimal. I'll be okay in a few days. Baby is fine. We got to hear her heartbeat. She looks like a little bean."

"That is so good to hear," he says. "I'm happy for you guys."

"You need to get Lana pregnant so I'm not alone," I say.

"I'll get right on that," he laughs and kisses me.

"You have a ring on," Nikolai says. I glance at my hand where the basic band they gave us, is.

"Elliot and I got married today," I say simply.

"Congratulations," he says with a smile. "So... Joshua did find one audio bug in the living room. It has since been destroyed. The rest of the house is clear."

"Thank you," I say.

"You're welcome," Nikolai says. "I'm glad you're okay."

"We are leaving tomorrow afternoon for a while. I just wanted you to know so you don't freak out if you try to look for me," I say.

"Going to see your Mom?"

"Yeah. How'd you know?"

"Because unfortunately, you're a lot like me with that. You'll never leave something alone unless you find closure a certain way. Just don't destroy yourself mentally if you don't hear what you are hoping for from her."

"She's a coward. She'll deny any wrongdoing or she'll make excuses for how she's the victim. She was a victim when Dad would beat the fuck out of her but the moment she walked away from me, knowing what was gonna happen she was no longer the victim," I say. "I guess Armen is not actually my dad, but whatever."

"I will handle Alexi while you all are gone then," he says.

"How? I'm getting really fucking tired of him and his stupid smile," I say.

"I'm going to kill him, Maya," he says. "I have given him every chance that I can. I have always tried to be patient with him, but he is defiant and honestly, he's a psychopath. He's always been devoid of emotion."

"What if he kills you?" I ask. "That's possible, right? If he kills you, I'm fucked. You are my last line of defense before he fucking butchers me for fun. If..." I abruptly stop talking when I realize that the thought of him dying is crushing. I don't know if it's because I am still trying to hold out hope for a parent that gives a fuck and he's been more supportive than the people who raised me. Even considering the sexual assault and kidnapping, he's been more of a Dad to me than the man I've called my Dad for twenty-five years. That's tragic, all things considered. I know I should not give a fuck if he dies or not. I should want to be the one to kill him, but for some stupid reason, I don't want him to die. I want him to keep trying to make amends with me, no matter how long that takes. The amount of genuine concern I've seen on his face in the last 24 hours is more than I ever saw from either of my parents. They did just enough to keep me alive, and that's it. Nikolai dropped everything to come help me tonight. He didn't have to do any of that. He didn't have to give a shit that his brother raped me again. Unlike most people, he has been willing to admit his fault.

"Maya," he says, putting his hands on my shoulders. "First of all, I appreciate that you're concerned for me, but don't be. I knew from the time I was a child that being a part of this world would lead to my demise. I'm glad you were never wrapped up in it and if I could do it over again, I would have done everything so much differently."

"I should hate you," I say quietly to hide my breaking voice. "I should want you dead."

"You should," he confirms. "And even though you understand the logic, you are still going to beat yourself up for caring."

"After what you did to me, I shouldn't want you to survive him... but he's done so much worse while you are trying to make up for what you did. My mother left me here knowing that you would find me one day. She knew you didn't know that I was yours and knew you'd come after me. She set me up. All of this could have been prevented if she had just told me the truth. You would have known the truth the very first day."

"You're rambling," he says softly.

"I know," I say as I close my eyes and sigh.

"Her and I have a lot of faults in this situation. Me, more than her, but fault nonetheless," he says as he tucks a stray hair behind my ear. "If this doesn't go the way I want it to and Alexi kills me, understand that he will come after you full force. Understand that the only way out of it is to kill him. if I die, and he gets a hold of you, you do whatever you can to kill him because he won't stop otherwise."

"I don't want you to die," I say as a rogue tear slips down my cheek. "I want you to spend the rest of your life, bugging the shit out of me to make amends."

"That's going to happen regardless of when I die, Maya," he says softly as he wipes away my tears. "Focus on you and that baby. Just don't be stubborn and not let them help you."

"Maya being stubborn? Not *her*," Daniel says, chuckling.

"Well, Mom is a leech that will suck you dry. So I

must get that from you," I say to Nikolai.

"It's a blessing and a curse," he says with a smile. "We are going to go but enjoy your trip. Okay?"

"We'll try," I say as we all walk to the door. I step out onto the porch with him. The others stay in the doorway while the doctor and Joshua go to the car.

"Try to minimize contact with me until I let you know he's been taken care of. I don't want him finding out that you are pregnant or where you are traveling to," Nikolai says.

"We'll be gone for a week."

"Okay. Be safe, please," he says.

Something inside of me tells me that this is the last time I will ever see him. It's as if my body can tell the future, but won't tell my brain exactly what it sees. I'll regret it if I don't do it and he actually dies. Before he can turn to go down the stairs, I hug him tightly. It takes him a second to react before he wraps his arms around me and hugs me back, resting his cheek on my head as he gently rubs my back. This connection is filled with so much emotion as if he knows that he'll never see me again either. No good will come from him confronting Alexi. For decades, Nikolai never had a soft spot. He never had a weak point for someone to use against him. Now he has me and I will be his demise.

"Get some sleep, Maya," he says softly before kissing the top of my head. I nod and step back so Elliot can put his arms around me. He pauses and looks at me for a moment before smiling. "You're already a wonderful Mother, Maya. She's lucky to have you two as parents."

"Bye, Nikolai," I say as I give up on hiding my emotions and note tears fall down my cheeks.

"Goodbye, Maya," he says with a kind smile before

turning and walking to the car.

These fucking hormones have me in a chokehold as I turn to Elliot and let him hold me as I fall apart. If they disagree with my decision to let him in my life as more than just an enemy, they don't show it. They all hug me as I cry, knowing something awful will happen. I don't know how I know, but I do.

Elliot picks me up and takes me to bed to lie down while Lana and Daniel lock up and join us. We go back to laying in the same position we were last night with Elliot behind me and Lana in front of me then Daniel behind her.

"I can't stop myself from caring about him," I sniffle.

"Maya, baby. You just found out today that he is your biological father, and now he's potentially about to sacrifice himself in the name of trying to get justice for you. He has been more of a parental figure in one day than your parents have your entire life. He will never be able to make up for what he did to you, but he is trying to do the right thing right now. You are not wrong for caring just as he is not wrong for wanting to make amends. If this is the last time you ever get to see him, know that it ended with him vowing to protect you no matter the outcome for him."

"Something bad is going to happen. I can feel it," I whisper.

"No matter what happens, we will be right here. We will always be right here," she says before kissing me. I relax into her before she pulls away. "Try to sleep, sweetie."

"I love you guys," I say after a moment of silence.

"We love you too, Maya," she says sweetly as she

pulls me close to lay my head on her chest. Elliot scoots in close to hold me and Daniel does the same for her.

Chapter Fifteen

Maya

Elliot let me sleep until shortly before we had to leave for the airport. Not only did I need the rest, but it was probably best. I didn't sit around the house and overthink.

We get to the airport in enough time to check our bags and get to the gate as they start the boarding process. Elliot got his first-class tickets so that I would have more room. I am sitting with Elliot while Daniel and Lana are sitting behind us. My mind is so preoccupied that I just put headphones in and listen to music for the entirety of the flight. When we land, I put them away and we all deboard the plane.

I am not looking forward to seeing Mom. Everything about her enrages me. These fucking hormones make all of my emotions ten times stronger than normal. When I get mad, I rage. When I get sad, I sob. I'll take it over throwing up though. I'm hoping morning sickness skips me.

When we get into the rental, I call Mom. I know she's not going to answer, but I keep calling anyway. I know where her mail was forwarded to, so we are going there first. It's about a twenty-minute drive from the airport to her house. She lives in a nice house that she bought with the insurance money when Armen died.

"Still nothing?" Lana asks.

"Nope," I say.

"Which one is her house?" Elliot asks as he slows down.

"Next one on the left. 115," I say, pointing to a white and blue house near the end of the road.

Elliot pulls into the driveway and I get out before anyone else and go to the door. Everyone else scrambles after me realizing that rage is the emotion I have chosen, going into this situation. I knock on the door and step back to wait. Elliot and Daniel are on either side of me and Lana is behind me.

Mom opens the door and goes wide-eyed when she sees me. She instantly goes to shut the door but I shove it open, pushing her backward. "Maya," she says. "What are you doing here?" She looks terrified and I know it has something to do with the two massive men standing with me. She's talked to Elliot, but she doesn't know that he looks like he could break her in half with little effort. He probably could, truth be told.

"Shouldn't you be asking if I'm okay? I know Elliot called you about me getting kidnapped," I say.

"I... How am I supposed to know what to say?" she asks.

"Sit," I say, pointing to her couch.

"I think it's best you leave," she says.

"*I think it's best you sit down and shut the fuck up,*" I yell at her. She simply nods and sits down.

"I should have known you'd get your father's rage," she says.

"Which one? Armen or Nikolai?" I ask with bitterness in my tone. "Because from where I sit, my father doesn't have any rage. In fact, he's the only one who seems to care about my well-being, even after assaulting me when he didn't know I was his daughter. You have amazing taste in men, Mom."

"Don't you judge me," she snaps. "Armen was awful to me."

"*And yet you stayed,*" I scream at her. "*You kept your only child in a place with the same man who fractured your skull because you burned dinner. You shoved me outside every day without a care in the world of what happened to me.*"

"You were fine. No one hurt you," she says, rolling her eyes.

"*Jonathan happened,*" I yell again. "He fucking latched onto me and sucked me in. I spent years being beaten and assaulted by him. I was held down and cut open more times than I can count. He sold me out to the fucking mafia when he found out Armen stole from Nikolai. Let's not forget that Elliot called you for help and you hung up on him. You knew I was in danger, and you didn't care."

"I did care. I didn't want you getting hurt but he would have fucking killed me, Maya. If he knew where I went, he'd kill me," she says tearfully.

"He knows where you are, you dumb bitch. He's not interested in killing you and never has been. He was interested in me. You could have prevented me getting violently raped twice by Alexi. This... my getting hurt over and over and over... that's your fault," I say.

"Alexi raped you?" she asks?

"Yeah. Once when I was kidnapped and then last night," I say. "Now, the man I should hate the most is about to potentially sacrifice himself to try and save me from Alexi. I should fucking despise him for what he did to me, but right now... he's the only person who's ever actually treated me like I'm his daughter. He cares more about me in one day than you ever did. Armen was fine when he wasn't drinking, but he hated my existence."

"I did the best I could," she frowns. "How dare you blame me for things I didn't do. I never hurt you."

"Your best?" I laugh. "God, you should have aborted me, you know that? You never should have been a parent."

The door comes open and a little girl about four years old barrels into the living room. "Mommy Mommy! Look! Daddy got me a new stuffie," she says as she launches herself into Mom's lap.

"Uh... That's nice honey. Why don't you take it to your room so Mommy can talk, huh?" she says sweetly.

"Okay, Momma," she says happily as she jumps down and runs down the hallway.

"Hey, Wendy," a man says as he leans down and kisses her. "Who are they?"

"I'm Maya," I say, offering him my hand.

"Don't, Maya," Mom warns.

"What? You don't want your new man to know you have a twenty-five-year-old daughter?" I ask before turning to the man. "I'm the daughter she abandoned in Nevada to start a new life here."

"Wendy, is this true?" he asks her. She hesitates for a moment and I know she's about to deny it. I can see it on her face.

"No. She must be mistaken," she says, unable to make eye contact with me suddenly. I can't help but laugh at her rejecting me openly.

"Yeah. I must be mistaken," I say flatly. "Congratulations on having a daughter. I know I am really excited to have my baby."

"You're pregnant?" she asks.

"Mhmm. We will get out of your hair, Wendy."

"Maya wait," she says, chasing after us. She catches my arm before I can get into the car.

"You are dead to me," I spin around and growl at her. "I hope you give that little girl a better life than you gave me. I hope she's happy and loved. Most of all... I hope she grows up and learns what a worthless cunt you are. Rot in hell, Wendy."

Elliot opens the door for me and I get in. Everyone else follows suit and we drive away, leaving Wendy standing in her driveway in shock. I lay my head back and take a deep breath.

"She looks like me," I say after a moment.

"Who?" Daniel asks.

"That little girl," I say. "She looks just like me at that age."

"Are you okay?" Elliot asks. "That's a lot to take in."

"Yeah, I'm okay. I didn't expect her to go and start a whole new family, but it doesn't surprise me. I just hope she's a better Mom to her than she was to me," I say.

"Fuck her," Lana says. "Let's go to the hotel and order some food."

"Food would be nice," I admit.

"What do you want to eat?" Daniel asks.

"Pizza," I answer. "Preferably with olives."

"That's disgusting," Elliot says, chuckling.

"Did you see what she was eating at the airport today?" Daniel asks Elliot and I giggle.

"I don't know if I want to know with her laughing like that," Elliot says.

"She got those mini dill pickles and a small thing of

peanut butter," Daniel says.

"Hey. You tried it and liked it," I point out.

"Okay... Yes... But it doesn't make it any less strange," he jokes.

"I'll give you that," I say with a smile.

We get to the beach house. I lay across the king-sized bed on my belly while Elliot and Daniel bring the bags inside.

"Pizza should be here soon," Lana says as she lies beside me. "Can I ask you something?"

"You can ask me anything," I say as I roll to my side to face her.

"The guys are too scared to ask you for fear of you thinking they are being pushy, but you know I don't care and I'll ask you what I want to know," she says. "Where is your head at with sex?"

"Outside of the obvious being off limits right now, I'm okay. I think I've been traumatized so much that I'm becoming desensitized to assault. Jonathan did it so often that it doesn't upset me anymore. It just makes me angry," I explain. "If I ever do become triggered though, I will speak up. I have always been vocal when saying no, even if no one listened."

"So if we wanted to give you your wedding present tonight?" she asks.

"I'm curious what that entails, but I'm okay with it," I say with a smile.

"Okay. Pizza then orgasms," she says as she pats my cheek and gets up from the bed.

I lie on the bed for a few more minutes before I hear the doorbell telling us that the pizza is here. I change into shorts and Elliot's T-shirt before I move out to the living room. Elliot hands me a plate of food when I sit on the couch. I eat my pizza while we all watch TV.

It's likely pregnancy related, but I am starting to thoroughly enjoy food. Everything we have been eating lately has been amazing. I'm hoping that this keeps up because I haven't had very many negative thoughts lately. It's nice to finally have energy for once. I was eating so little before and working out so hard, causing me to feel weak most of the day. I haven't gone to the gym once since I left Jonathan and I've been eating more often. I have gained weight, but my face is less sunken in than it was before, so I think I am simply gaining back what I should have had to begin with. I may feel differently after pregnancy, but I'll take it as a win for now. I know I can't go overboard or it'll throw me back into the deep end again with my eating disorder.

When I get done eating I take everyone's paper plates to the trash. "Maya, come here," Lana calls out from somewhere in the house.

"Where are you?" I ask.

"Bedroom." I laugh and walk to the bedroom.

"You really did mean right after supper," I laugh.

"Sure did," she says as she points for me to sit on the bed. "Where is your head?"

"Just curious what you two are up to," I say.

"Alright. Daniel is going to lead. Keep your focus on him," she says as Daniel pulls me back to lie before moving me to the end of the bed so that my head dangles off the bed some.

"Ready for me, Maya," Daniel asks before leaning down to kiss me.

"Always," I say happily.

I open up for him as he pushes himself down my throat. His pace starts slow and is gradually picking up with each stroke. He pulls my shirt up to expose my breasts so he can tease my nipples with pinches and gentle caresses. Lana pulls at my shorts and I lift my hips so she can pull them off of me, taking my underwear with them.

Just as I am realizing what she is going to do, Daniel's pace doubles and he starts fucking my throat hard and fast. I am so distracted by Daniel that Lana spreading my legs doesn't register until she gently licks across my clit.

I moan around Daniel as she flicks her tongue across me so precisely that I involuntarily push my hips toward her. Daniel moves his hands to my face as he fucks my face faster. I have my hands on the back of his thighs and I am gripping onto him as Lana absolutely ravages me with her mouth. I knew this woman was amazing, but goddamn, she know how to work my body.

I am hollowing my cheeks, sucking Daniel down. The feeling of her tongue on me is so overwhelming that it's all I can do to keep myself still. She has her hands pressing on my inner thighs to keep me spread for her. Daniel groans as he pushes to the back of my throat and comes. I greedily drink him down as my orgasm builds.

When he pulls out of my mouth my moans become audible. "Fuck," I cry out.

"God you take her tongue so well, my sweet little slut. Come for my wife, Maya. Scream for her" Daniel says to me quietly as he teases my nipples.

Lana sucks on my clit hard and my entire body starts to shake. "Oh my God, I'm gonna come," I moan loudly. When it hits me, I arch dramatically as sounds I've never heard before flood out of me.

Long after the sensations fade away she releases

me and I sink into the mattress. "Dear God, woman," I groan as she comes up to me. I grab her face and kiss her, tasting my arousal on her tongue.

I let instinct take over and roll us to where I am on top. We are still lost in our kiss when Elliot grabs my hips and pulls me back to the edge of the bed. As he moves me closer to him I kiss down her chest and abdomen, then pull off her shorts. She eagerly parts her legs for me and I settle between her thighs. As Elliot slowly slides into me I bury my face in her cunt. When my tongue makes contact with her, she gasps and arches her back.

Elliot grips my waist and surges into me over and over, making me groan. He is pulling an orgasm up so quickly that I can't keep my focus on Lana so I suck on her clit as I push two fingers into her. She is fisting my hair and her little whimpers are intoxicating. The harder Elliot fucks me, the harder I fuck Lana. I curl my fingers in and she screams out as her legs start to shake.

"Fuck. Oh God, Maya. Yes! Just like that," she begs. I keep my same pace and she starts to unravel for me. I nip and suck her through her orgasm until she pulls away from me.

Elliot pauses to pull me off the bed to my feet and Lana moves to sit on the bed directly in front of me. Elliot bends me over to where my hands on are either side of her and my head is on her chest. He slams into me and I push back to force him deeper inside of me. I hear the buzz of a toy right before Lana reaches between my legs and presses a wand massager to my clit.

I instantly scream out as pleasure takes over my body again and I come. Neither of them let up and I am reduced to whimpers and pleas for more. "Keep coming, Maya," Lana whispers in my ear as I groan.

"Fuck," I whimper. "God, it's too much."

"You can do it, baby. Keep coming for us," she encourages. Elliot is fucking me and insanely fast. The intensity of everything has my body tensing as I fall into back-to-back orgasms. When Elliot starts to moan, Lana starts grinding the wand against my clit. As Elliot comes, they both force a climax from me that makes my breath catch and my legs nearly buckle.

By the time Elliot pulls out of me I am exhausted and satisfied. He moves me to lie on the bed so she can clean me and help me back into my shorts. I move to lie in the middle of the bed with Lana as the guys take their positions behind us. Almost immediately I fall asleep snuggled between Lana and Elliot.

Chapter Sixteen

Maya

One Week Later

We spent our entire week going to the beach and various attractions that Lana had planned for us. This has been the most stress-free I have been in an extremely long time. It was nice to get my mind off of everything for once. Although, they kept us so busy that I didn't have time to think about much else. If we weren't running around doing something, we were sleeping or fucking.

Late last night, Lana woke me up and dragged me to the store with her to buy a pregnancy test when she realized that she should have started a few days after I was due. When we got back to the beach house, the guys were awake and suspicious of where we went. When she told Daniel that she thought she was pregnant, he laughed. His only response was "We should have thought this through before knocking you both up at the same time."

When she finally took the test it was positive, which will put her at about five weeks pregnant. I am so excited that I'll be going through this with her so neither of us is alone.

Lana and I spend the entire flight back talking about baby stuff and our plans to raise them together.

Elliot and Daniel seem equally as excited about this. We are all still worried about the Alexi situation since I have yet to hear from Nikolai.

Part of me is holding out hope that Nikolai is okay and Alexi is taken care of, but I know better. Alexi has Ivan on his side and God knows who else. I want to just pack up and run, but I know it won't help. Alexi will find me no matter where I go. He will keep reminding me of my place, and I pray I find a solution before he finds out that I am pregnant.

We have discussed going to the FBI and asking for help. Surely they'd help me outrun the Russian mafia somehow. I know if I got caught going to the cops I would die much quicker than they could help me, so that is an absolute last resort.

When we get our bags from baggage claim, we make our way to Elliot's car. It's getting late in the evening now, so I want to just eat and go to sleep. Tomorrow we have to go into the office for a few meetings and Elliot wants to move me into the position of his partner, rather than his assistant. I am confident in my ability to get the hang of things, but there will be a learning curve.

We get loaded up and start driving toward the house. I am nearly asleep when my phone goes off. I gasp and sit up in my seat when I see that it's Nikolai texting me.

"Thank God," I say.

"Nikolai?" Elliot asks.

"Yeah," I say as I open the text.

Nikolai: Everything is taken care of. When you get into town, come by the house so we can all talk about what happened.

Me: We just got in. Give us a few and we will be there.

Nikolai: See you soon.

"He wants to tell us what happened and asked for us to come by," I say.

"We can't be long. You need to get some sleep," he says, kissing my hand.

"I know. I just want to see him, which I know sounds dumb as hell."

"It's not dumb, Maya," Lana says. "Nothing about this situation is conventional. You are allowed to have your feelings however you wish to feel them. We know you aren't excusing what he did, but he and the three of us are the only ones looking out for your well-being. You have the right to hope he's okay."

I am nervous and fidgety for the entire drive to Nikolai's house. Something in my gut is telling me to run away, but I push that feeling down over and over until we pull past the gate to his house.

The lights are on and everything appears to be normal for a mafia house. Nikolai's usual car is parked up front. There is no sign of anyone outside, so that is comforting enough for us to get out of the car. Elliot comes around the car to hold my hand as we walk up to the door.

"Something is off," I say as we stop in front of the door. Everything is too quiet.

Before anyone can respond to me, the door comes open and I see Alexi with his stupid smile standing in the doorway. We all back up and turn to rush back to the car only to be faced with Ivan and Jonathan with guns drawn.

"It's nice of you to join us, Maya. I didn't think you'd fall for it," Alexi says as he grabs me by the hair and pulls me into the house. Jonathan and Ivan nudge the others into the house with us. Ivan has me facing the others and I see a look of dread cross their faces when they glance behind us into the living room.

"You don't have to do this, Alexi," I say through my tears.

"You're right, I don't have to... But I want to," Alexi says as Ivan and Jonathan zip-tie Elliot, Daniel, and Lana's hands behind their backs. They are all focused on me and rightfully keeping their mouths shut. It will only make things worse for me if they talk.

"What was it you said about killing me?" Jonathan asks as he comes around to stand in front of me.

"Fuck you," I snap at him. Jonathan slaps me across the face so hard that my ears ring.

"I think it's time to see the mess you've made, huh?" Alexi says.

He turns and shoves me to the ground while Ivan forces the others to stand along the wall. When I look up I see Nikolai tied to a chair. He is beaten badly and has tape over his mouth. His eyes are nearly swollen shut and he has dried blood on his face and chest.

I cover my mouth to keep my cries silent. I know he is about to kill him in front of me. He wants to make this hurt as much as possible. He is dazed but grief floods his face when he looks up and sees me on the floor. Tears fall down his cheeks as he starts to weep.

Alexi rips the tape off his mouth and throws it to the floor before walking around behind him. "Please... Let her go, brother. This is between you and me," Nikolai mutters.

"You chose your whore of a daughter over the empire we built. You were ready to throw it all away to get on her good side," Alexi says as he grabs him by the hair and pulls his head back.

"Please, let her go," Nikolai pleads.

"Any last words, Nikolai?" Alexi asks as he flips a knife open and puts it to his throat.

I pick myself up from the floor and Jonathan promptly wraps his arm around my waist to keep me from interfering.

"I'm so sorry, dochka. I wish we had more time," Nikolai says. "I tried to save you." Alexi smiles at me as drags the knife across Nikolai's throat, slicing it open. Nikolai makes a slight gurgling sound as he starts to bleed out.

"*No!*" I scream and fight against Jonathan to try and get to Nikolai, to try and save him. Grief takes over when Nikolai slumps in his chair and Alexi lets go of his head. I bring myself to my knees as I sob for the little girl who dreamed of having a Dad to take care of her. All of my tears are for my little girl who will know a world without him as a protector. No matter how fucked up in the head he was, he cared about me. He tried to save me... to save us. I have never felt so sure of my death as I do right now.

"Get up," Alexi says as he walks over to me. When I don't obey him, Jonathan grabs me by the hair and pulls me up to stand.

"*Fuck you!*" I scream at him as I shove him before Jonathan can stop me. Alexi promptly grabs me by the throat and slams me up against a nearby wall.

"If you don't want to watch me do the same things to them, I'd advise you to be a good little whore and obey me when I speak," Alexi growls. "Got it?" I nod and he lets go of my throat.

"Everyone in the basement," Alexi says. "Ivan, sit them along the wall. I'll take care of Maya." When I look at the others, they have tape over their mouths. They all look like they are stuck between grief and rage, just like me.

Alexi grabs me by the arm and drags me toward the basement. I know better than to hesitate with Alexi. I know he will hurt me worse than Jonathan ever has. He pulls me down the stairs with the others behind us. When we get to the bottom, he stops me in front of a table.

"Here's how this is going to work, puppet," Alexi says as Ivan and Jonathan start cutting my clothes off. "If you disobey me, one of them dies. If you say anything other than 'Yes, Master' you will be whipped. If you piss me off, I will get rid of that leech of a baby you are carrying. Got it?"

"Speak up, Maya," Jonathan says with humor in his voice before smacking my ass. "We can't hear you."

"Yes, Master," I say through gritted teeth.

"Good girl," Alexi smiles. "Now get on your knees and show us how much you want to keep that baby." I glance over at Elliot with tears in my eyes. He nods, telling me to comply with Alexi's orders. I sniff back my tears as I come down to my knees.

Alexi holds my wrists behind my head with one hand as he pulls his erection out. "Watch the teeth," he commands. Just before he pushes himself into my mouth, he pauses. "Tsk tsk, silly puppet. What do you say?"

"Yes, Master," I whisper.

"Good girl," he says as he thrusts himself into my mouth. He immediately finds a pace that has him face fucking me with so much force that I can't breathe. He never lets up as he pushes himself further down my throat with each stroke. My jaw and throat ache at the way he is using my mouth to steal his pleasure. It doesn't take him long to shove himself down as far as he can reach as he comes.

When he pulls out of my mouth I fall to my hands coughing and gasping for air. I am offered no reprieve as Jonathan grabs me by the hair to pull me up. "Fight me and I'll cut that fucking thing out of you," Jonathan says as he forces his way down my throat. He too finds an unrelenting speed at which he cuts off my airway, not allowing me to breathe. He groans obnoxiously loud as he fucks my mouth. As always, he doesn't last long. When he shoves himself deep into my mouth, he pinches my nose closed to ensure that I swallow.

As soon as he pulls out of me, Ivan swoops in and I hardly get a full breath before he sets in on taking his pleasure with my mouth. Ivan uses brute force behind his thrusts. His body odor combined with how deep into my throat he is pushing forces me to gag. I try to coax myself out of throwing up because I know he won't stop. I will end up choking on my own vomit while he continues to fuck my throat. He continues to rapidly pump himself in and out of my mouth until he finally pushes deep and comes.

Ivan then grabs me by the hair and drags me toward the Saint Andrew's cross where Alexi and Jonathan put me on display across the room from Elliot, Daniel, and Lana. They all have a very clear look of rage in their eyes as they keep their attention focused on me.

"We will be back a little later," Alexi says. "Be a good girl."

"Yes, Master," I say again through gritted teeth.

Before they leave, they pull the tape off of their mouths. None of us talk, even after the basement door shuts. We all know they can hear us.

"Are you okay?" Elliot asks, breaking the silence.

"I'm okay," I say quietly.

"I'm sorry he made you see that," Lana says tearfully.

"I... I don't even know how to process that. I knew it would be bad but..."

"I know," she says. "All you can do right now is comply. I don't know if they will spare you or us, but it's the only thing to do right now."

"Yeah. Fighting will only get me hurt," I say. "Somehow being degraded and taunted like that is worse." I know they're listening, so I'm hoping they take my words and choose to shame and degrade me rather than cause me pain.

Lana perks up, realizing what I'm doing. "Whatever you do, just don't let yourself get off if they rape you. They'll attach to that shit and use it against you." Daniel and Elliot give her a strange look until I continue.

"Yeah. I know. I'd almost take getting hurt over that shit. It fucks with my head and just feels icky."

"Well, just don't come and you won't have a problem," Daniel says with feigned annoyance in his voice. Leave it to him to be the one to make a smartass comment. I don't know if they're watching also, so I keep a straight face.

"I don't have control over that, Daniel," I say, trying to fake an attitude.

"You do have a choice, Maya. You did last time too and still let it happen," Elliot says. I can see in his eyes that he wants to smile at me. I know they are all bullshitting me.

My hope is that they will latch onto this idea that forced orgasms is worse than brutally and violently raping me. If they think it's more fun for them to torture me with that, then I can be spared pain and damage.

"Whatever, Elliot," I sigh and lay my head back.

We all go back to being silent for a while. We don't want to say too much and end up getting one or all of us hurt. Hopefully, the plan works and they resort to just making me come on repeat. It still fucking sucks. It still makes me feel like my insides are lava. My brain is screaming at my body to stop but it doesn't. It keeps sending me into orgasm after orgasm. Maybe if I relaxed it would feel okay, but there is no way I'd be able to relax, even if only for a second. If I relax, I'll probably throw up.

I am terrified of Ivan assaulting me. No matter what he does, it's going to hurt. Luckily they all seem to be finishing quickly today, so maybe it won't get too violent. The basement door opens and I flinch and lift my head so I can see them coming at me.

"Hello," Alexi says with a smile. As he stands in front of me. "Would you like to play with me, puppet?" I close my eyes for a moment and bang my head back against the wood.

"Yes, Master," I say almost inaudibly.

"Speak up, puppet," he says with a kind voice. It's a trap, I know it.

"Yes. Master." I spit out.

"Good choice," he says, glancing at the others and grinning. "Tell me... who's better at eating that tight little cunt of yours?"

I keep my mouth shut because I feel like he's trying to trick me.

"You can answer, puppet," he says.

"Lana," I reply.

"Hell, I didn't know you were a carpetmuncher, Maya," Jonathan laughs.

"Here's how we will do this then," Alexi says. "You make a single sound and you'll watch me fuck her just like I did to you in that bathroom. Do you understand?"

"Yes, Master," I say reluctantly. There is no fucking way I'm letting Lana get raped. I look at her and she is back to being in tears.

"Any of you say a single word or make a sound, I'll gut her in front of you," Alexi says to the others before stepping closer to me. "If I ask you a question, you may still reply with "yes, master" only. Otherwise, I don't want to hear anything coming from you. Got it?"

"Yes, Master," I say stiffly with hatred in my voice.

When Alexi goes to his knees in front of me I grit my teeth and bang my head against the wood of the cross again. My plan worked, but a little too well. He spreads me open for him before softly licking across my clit. I close my eyes and focus everything on not making a sound. His tongue on me forces a different feeling. With the slickness of his mouth combined with soft touches, my body is reacting exactly the way he wants. The sensations that he is creating should feel nice, but they are nauseating.

"My sweet little puppet, I should have sampled this pretty little pussy a long time ago," he says. Alexi thrusts his tongue inside of me before dragging it across my clit with pressure behind his touch. My body flinches when he flicks across me and he chuckles. "Keep quiet, puppet."

Alexi sucks my clit into his mouth and suddenly my whole body is on fire. I hold my breath and lay my head back to focus on anything besides how my body is screaming for a release, pulsating and begging for more but I don't want more. I want him to go away. I want him to stop touching me. My body is doing more than betraying me, it's begging him for more.

My thighs are shaking as an intense orgasm builds. Alexi pushes three fingers inside of me and starts to fuck me, pounding against my G-spot. "You're so wet for me. Do you want your uncle to make you come now, puppet?"

"Yes, Master," I say, nearly growling.

"I can't hear you, Maya," he says before nipping my clit with his teeth, making me flinch.

"Yes, Master," I say louder.

"Louder, whore. Do you want me to make you come?"

"Yes, Master," I nearly scream as he sucks on me harder while he nips gently. Alexi curls his fingers in as he fucks me harder and harder. Suddenly everything peaks and smashes down as an orgasm gut punches me. A groan forces its way out as he continues to suckle on me. When he finally lets up, I sag on the cross.

"Tsk tsk, puppet. You weren't supposed to make any noise," he says as he stands up in front of me. "Don't worry, I'll still be fucking you."

When Alexi turns and walks toward Lana and she bursts into tears, I fold immediately. "Stop. Please stop," I cry. Alexi slowly turns to face me with a conniving grin on his face.

"You are one brave little bitch, Maya. You would get yourself whipped just so I won't touch her?"

"Yes, Master," I say tearfully. "Please don't. I'll do whatever you want me to do. Please don't hurt her."

Alexi watches me for a second, thinking. Lana is

still sobbing while Daniel and Elliot are raging angry. "I'll make you a deal," he says as he comes over to me. He unhooks my restraint as he explains. "If you agree to willingly walk yourself over to that table and let us all fuck you at once, no one will touch them."

"Okay," I say immediately.

"You would climb into Ivan's lap and let him and Jonathan fuck you just to spare Lana?"

"Yes," I say without hesitation. There's no fucking way. I'm letting them hurt her. Over my dead body. I will take on whatever I have to to ensure that none of them get hurt.

"Fine," he says. "If you don't come for us, I'll fuck her bloody and unconscious. Got it?"

"Yes, Master," I cry.

"Good girl, puppet," he says, patting my cheek.

"Ivan. Jonathan. Use lube and make the whore beg for it. I want Elliot and Daniel to see how good you can make her feel."

"You got it, boss," Ivan grins before moving to the table. It's sitting low enough, like a coffee table, that I won't have to do much climbing. Alexi nudges me toward him and I willingly walk closer, knowing he will hurt her if I don't comply. Lana's cries keep me walking closer.

Ivan slathers lube all over his dick as he watches me walk to him. Eventually, I get close enough where Ivan can easily lift me and bring me into his lap. I expect him to slam inside of me but he slowly lowers me onto him, gradually filling me. "We want to hear everything this time, puppet. Let us hear the way you scream through your orgasm."

Ivan is tightly gripping my hips to guide me as he slowly fucks me. The nauseating feeling returns when my body responds to the forced feelings. When a small moan slips free, he lays back and pulls me down with him. "Such a tight little cunt," Ivan growls. He has my arms crossed in front of my chest with his arms wrapped around my abdomen so that my face is buried in his chest. When he starts to fuck me harder, I unwillingly groan. This only fuels him and he dives deeper into me, forcing more disgusting sounds from me. The silver lining to the vile unwanted pleasure that he is forcing on me is that I'm not in pain. As long as I am not in pain, my baby is safe. I keep thinking of her and the person she will grow up to be. Compliance is the only way out of this, just let them take what they want. We will have an opening eventually to get away. They haven't taken anything from them, so Elliot still has the keys in his pocket.

An orgasm sweeps over me, forcing moans from me. Ivan stays buried in me as Jonathan slicks himself down and rapidly fills me with his erection. They immediately find a rhythm where they are alternating strokes deep inside of me. Just as an orgasm is about to flood my body, Jonathan groans and comes.

Alexi immediately takes his place and slams into me. Jonathan's approach prepared me well enough that I am not in pain. He pulls me up against his chest before wrapping his hand around my throat to hold me in place. He and Ivan move in and out of my body with a feverish need to come inside me as Alexi has his other hand gripping my hip.

At this point, there is no sense in fighting or dulling what they're doing to me. I let my body react however it chooses and I will sort the emotions later. I am panting as my body is begging for release. Jonathan comes forward and with slicked fingers, starts running them against my clit. "Tell them you want it harder," Alexi growls. I don't respond at first and he tightens his grip on my throat.

"I want it harder," I choke out.

"Louder," Alexi barks.

"Harder," I say with tears streaming down my face as they turn frenzied as they fuck me

"Again," he demands loudly. He uses my impending orgasm as fuel to get what he wants from me. He wants to think I'm begging for it.

"*Harder,*" I scream. I just want him to shut up. He knows he is forcing me so my words mean nothing. He knows I'm not willing. I think he likes the fact that I don't want this and is using that power over me.

"Come for me, puppet," he whispers in my ear as he bites my neck and tightens his grip on my throat. I don't have a chance to react to not being able to breathe before my orgasm rips through me. Everything I'm feeling together is overwhelming. Pressure doesn't stop as they continue to pound into me. I start to panic when I feel it coming on. The orgasm won't stop building up to a larger climax. I still can't breathe. I suddenly and silently come so hard that I see stars. Just as my vision starts to tunnel and my body unwillingly relaxes, he releases his grip on my throat. The second oxygen floods my lungs, I scream out as my forced arousal floods out of me and soaks Ivan and the table below.

They both groan loudly and get dragged down with me into their release. When they pull out of me, Ivan stands, turns, and drops me onto the table to lie across it. Jonathan pulls my hands above my head to restrain them to the table while Ivan and Alexi collect themselves. They tie my ankles to the table before Jonathan abruptly walks away and goes up the basement steps.

I look over at Elliot, Daniel, and Lana. They look like they are ready to kill someone. When Jonathan comes back down to the basement, panic floods me when I see he has a wire coat hanger.

"No. Jonathan, no. Please don't do this. Please don't," I beg. "Please. I'm begging you. Don't do this to me."

None of them say anything in response to my begging. They just chuckle. They have their backs to the others as they stand beside me. John maintains eye contact with me as he straightens the coat hanger out into one piece of metal.

"Stop. Please stop. Please don't do this," I scream when he drags the end of the wire across my inner thigh.

"This baby in your belly should be mine, Maya," Jonathan says. "You have two options. I either carve this baby out of you so I can put my own in you, or you all die right now."

"Please don't do this to me," I sob.

"Pick, Maya. If I have to pick, I'm going to scrape out this baby before killing them at your feet. You will watch the light leave their eyes as you bleed out your baby," he says coolly before screaming at me. "*Pick, Maya.*"

I'm crying so hard that I can't form any words. How am I supposed to pick between the two? I have hesitated for too long, and Jonathan laughs. "Say goodbye to your baby, Maya," he says.

As he slowly drags the wire hanger down my abdomen, Daniel, Elliot, and Lana start screaming. I am so lost in my panic that I can't focus on the words they are saying. I am desperately pulling at my restraints to try to free myself as I sob hysterically.

Right as he is about to shove the piece of metal

inside of me, he drops to the ground. Elliot and Daniel have a murderous look in their eye as they quickly and swiftly take down Ivan and Alexi. I'm suddenly thrust into shock and I start screaming.

I don't know why I am screaming at the top of my lungs, but it's the only release I can find for the panic that is still swirling inside of me. I can see that I'm safe, but my brain doesn't believe it. It's still waiting for the pain and the grief to stab through me. Elliot takes my restraints off as Daniel restraints the others. Elliot pulls me off the table and cradles me in his arms before bringing himself to sit against the wall with me in his lap. Daniel moves over to Lana to get her restraints off before they all come over to surround me.

"We've got you. You're okay," Elliot says over and over, as if trying to convince himself of my survival.

"Shhh. You're okay, Maya. Breathe," Lana encourages. "It's over. You're safe now."

Elliot gently rocks me while I force myself to calm down and stop sobbing.

"Someone find her something to wear," Elliot says.

"There is a bedroom up the stairs at the end of the hall. That's the one Nikolai had me in. There should be clothing in there," I say, wiping back my tears. Lana jumps up and races up the stairs.

"Are you okay? How do you feel?" Daniel asks.

"Stupid," I say.

"Why?" Elliot asks.

"I don't know. I knew what was going to happen. I knew what they would do when we started saying all that when they were upstairs... I guess I just didn't expect to react to it like that," I say as Elliot wipes the tears from my face.

"I'm just glad they didn't hurt you," Elliot says before kissing me softly.

"I'm so angry," I say. "They should die for what they've done to me."

"What do you want to do?" Daniel asks.

"I want to burn this house to the ground with them in it," I admit.

"I won't say no, but we are talking about murder, Maya," Elliot says seriously. "Can you live with yourself if you do this?"

"I have to live with what they did to me for the rest of my life. I can live with being the one to rid the world of them," I say as Lana comes down into the basement.

"Come on. They're waking up. Let's get you dressed," Lana says as she pulls me up from the ground.

"How did you guys get free?" I ask Elliot and Daniel.

"They went full-on Hulk when he was about to hurt you with that coat hanger," Lana says as she helps me step into shorts.

"I can't believe he was going to do that," I say, pulling a shirt over my head. One at a time, Alexi, Ivan, and Jonathan wake up. Alexi groans as they all lift their heads to look around. They are dazed, especially Jonathan. Elliot punched him directly in the back of the head when he knocked him out. I'm surprised he's even awake right now.

"You stupid bitch," Jonathan mutters.

"Shut the fuck up, Jonathan," I snap at him before turning to Elliot. "How do I do this?"

"Turn the gas to the stove on and light one of the curtains on fire. That'll give us time to get away before everything blows," he says.

"Oh. We are killing them?" Lana asks.

"What?" Alexi asks. "You can't do that."

"I can and I will," I say with a deadpan expression.

"Maya, you are not a killer," he says.

"Oh, are we on a first-name basis now? What happened to being your puppet?" I ask as I slip my feet back into my sandals that were carelessly thrown across the room. I go to my tattered shorts and get my phone out of the pocket. "Never thought I'd see the day where I outsmarted you, Alexi."

"If you kill me, everyone will be coming after you," Alexi growls.

"*No, I got revenge for Nikolai,*" I scream at him. "You murdered a Russian mafia boss in front of his daughter. Do you think you would have survived after that? He knew what was going to happen. He walked away from me, knowing *exactly* what you were going to do to him. You don't think he had something in place to make sure you went down for it?"

"You don't know him. He was corrupt," he says. I kick him in the chest and he falls on his back with his arms pinned under him.

"He was the only family I had and you took that from me. I had a chance to have a real parent and you slaughtered him," I say as I start to cry.

"He forced you to suck his dick but suddenly now he's daddy of the year?" Alexi laughs and I kick him in the ribs making him groan.

"*I am the only one who gets to judge him for what he did to me,*" I yell. "*He fucked up, but he tried. He tried to make it right. He tried to undo all the bad he did and you killed him for it. You killed him for trying to be a good person.*"

"Maya," Elliot says softly. "Let's go."

I nod and wipe my tears before turning to

Jonathan. For the first time, he's learned to keep his mouth shut. "I told you that I would be the death of you," I say simply.

We all walk toward the stairs and I turn back to look at the trio, bound and lying on the floor. They're silent and fear paints their face.

"Maya, we can work something out here," Jonathan says with sadness in his voice. "You've known me your entire life. Come on. Please don't do this."

"That's what I said when you were about to abort my baby," I say.

"Maya, please. This is insane," Jonathan pleads.

"Give it up. She's just like her Father," Alexi mutters.

"Burn in hell, *Master*" I spit out as we walk up the basement stairs. When we get to the top, we shut and barricade the door before turning the gas for the stove wide open.

When we get to the living room, I go to where Nikolai's body is still slumped in the chair. I gently touch the top of his head and I can't stop the flood of tears. "I forgive you," I whisper. "You tried to do better and be a good father to me. You sacrificed yourself to give me a chance at survival. Your debt has been paid, Nikolai. You'll always be my father, no matter our past."

I wipe my tears and turn to the others, who are also in tears. "Ready?" Elliot asks me.

"Yeah," I say. "Let's burn it down."

"You guys go," Daniel says. "I'll set the fire. It's easier for one to get out rather than all of us at once.

"Daniel," I sigh.

"No. You are pregnant and you've been through a lot tonight, go to the car," He says firmly. I nod and kiss him as Elliot pushes Lana and me out of the door. We get into the car and Elliot has it shifted into gear while we wait on Daniel. As soon as we see the curtain catch, Daniel darts out of the door and jumps in. He doesn't even have the door shut before Elliot peels out of the driveway.

A deafening roar comes up from behind us, shaking the car. When I turn back the house seems to dissipate before my eyes. Bits of rubble are raining down from the explosion. We don't stop driving, even though we know that the response time for fire and rescue this far out in the desert is laughable. When our tires hit the pavement, Elliot stomps on the gas to put as much distance between us and the blast.

I lie my head back and close my eyes. All of my fears and trauma just went up in flames with that house and it makes me feel lighter suddenly. I know I have a lot to overcome with my mental health but without Jonathan, Alexi, and Ivan out of the picture, I can finally heal.

For my entire life, I was held captive in the shadows of my trauma. I defined myself based on what others did to me and allowed it to control my every move. From this day forward, I will create an environment where my little girl will never doubt the love her father and I have for her. We will raise her to be strong and independent, but also self-aware of her mental health. She will have an understanding that asking for help is okay and accepting abuse from others is not.

Epilogue

Ten Years Later

It's hard to believe it's been ten years since the explosion... Since Nikolai was murdered. I think about that time of my life often and I will always remember how lucky I was to have Nikolai protecting me. When I first met him, he was a nightmare that had come to life. Everything changed when I found out that he was my father. The news of him having a daughter shook his world and made him see the things he was doing for what they really were. I was so reluctant to accept him because he assaulted me. I couldn't fathom the thought of forgiving him for what he did to me... For what he was planning on doing to me.

Everything changed the night Alexi cornered me in the bathroom. Nikolai dropped everything to come to me, then sacrificed himself to give me a fighting chance at survival. I was so clouded by the trauma of the night he died that it was hard for me to see the full picture of what he did for me.

The day after the explosion, I went to the hospital to get checked out. I was having some cramping and wanted to be sure that she was okay. I knew they'd want to do a rape kit, but I denied it so no one would ask questions. I knew I couldn't give a name or that would connect all of us to the explosion, but it didn't matter.

Once they checked to make sure I was okay and the baby was okay, a detective visited us. To this day, I have no idea how they knew to come talk to me, but I suspect that they already had caught wind of my involvement with that family.

The man asked me why I was denying the rape kit and I simply told him that I wanted to move on with my life. That wasn't a lie. I just wanted to move on and heal. I knew this was possible because we murdered the ones who were hellbent on destroying me. The detective asked various questions about Nikolai and Alexi, but I kept my answers vague. I didn't confirm or deny that I was raped by Alexi, Ivan, and Jonathan, but I did make a point to say that Nikoli was innocent and he has nothing to do with my attack.

The detective told me that four bodies were found in the rubble of the house, one of which died from a cut to the throat. He didn't go into detail on how they knew Nikolai was the one who was murdered, but he told me he knew that, for once, Nikolai was innocent. He explained that Nikolai had halted all shipments and was in the process of abruptly ending his involvement in any of the illegal affairs he had previously been a part of. I remembered that Alexi said he was about to essentially dismantle everything for me, so the knowledge of him working toward being on the right side of the law solidified for me that he was making an honest effort to do right by me.

Before the detective left, he told me that there were too many different variables to what could have happened in the basement, so the murders were likely going to end up going unsolved. Ultimately, the cause of the fire was determined to be an accident due to a candle lighting a curtain on fire. I asked what that meant and he told me that whoever was the one that tied the three men up in the basement would get away with murder because the department didn't have the funds to allocate resources toward the investigation.

The look he gave me told me it was clear that he knew I was involved but essentially did not care. I wiped out an entire mafia family with one explosion. All of the lower-level people Nikolai had working for him disappeared, so the Pavlov crime family was extinct.

Roughly three months later, I was approached by Nikolai's lawyer. He told me that shortly before his death he had something written up so that if anything happened to him, all of his assets were to be liquidated and given to me as an inheritance. I knew that he was well off, but I did not expect that inheritance to be seventy-five million dollars.

When he told me the number, I stared at him in silence for upwards of five minutes while Elliot asked a thousand different questions about the money. We were assured that the money was clean and we would not run into any issues. It took me a minute to process everything before I finally accepted the check.

Before we left, he handed me an envelope with my name on it and told me that Nikolai had left it for me if anything were to happen to him. I asked if he knew what was in it, and he said that all Nicolai would tell him was I would understand the semblance of what he was giving me.

I held onto that envelope until the day I had my daughter. I wasn't ready to face his words just yet, but looking into my little girl's eyes for the first time, I knew I needed to read it. Elliot, Daniel, and Lana sat with me while I read it aloud to them.

Maya,

If you are reading this, it is because I was successful in saving you. I suspect you have many questions, so I will do my best to answer them here.

I know that choosing you over the organization I built would mean I would be signing my death certificate. I have the choice right now to give in and allow Alexi to take you out however he chooses, or slow him down enough to ensure that you survive him after I die. The decision to pick you was natural and not something I have doubted myself about. You deserve to live a long and happy life with your partners. Your daughter deserves to meet her strong-willed and courageous mother. She deserves to know the love you have dreamed of your entire life. My decision ensures that you all get to live that dream free from the world I created.

I am leaving you with everything I have to offer. I know it doesn't take back what I have done to you and what I allowed, but know that I will spend the rest of my life regretting what I have done. "I'm sorry" isn't enough. You deserve more, so this is me trying to make up for what I have done and the pain I have caused you. I hope that we get more time together so that I can show you just how much you mean to me in the short time I've known you. If we are not given more time, understand that everything I am doing right now is for you and your little girl. Staying alive means nothing if you are not here as well.

I wish I had a lifetime worth of todays, so I could spend every moment learning to love you more. You will be my daughter until my dying breath and beyond.

I love you more than this letter will ever be able to express.

> **Until we meet again,**
> **Nikolai**

Inside the envelope were two identical necklaces. The pendant is of three roses with a black snake intertwining its stems, all braided by vines. On the back, there is one word engraved that embodies everything Nikolai gave me. Hope.

Elliot and I named our little girl Viktoriya Nicole Greene. We wanted her name to mean something, so we chose to give her a name that means "victory" and has a Russian spelling to honor Nikolai. Although, lately she prefers to be called Riya. She is directly named after him with her middle name being Nicole and we have made sure she knows who she is named after.

With her only being nine, we leave out the gory details of his death and just tell her that he died saving her and me. We have explained to her that her grandfather did bad things but in the end, when it mattered, he chose to do the right thing without hesitation. She seems to accept that answer for now. When she's much older we will explain the full story, minus her mom and dad murdering three people.

Lana and Daniel had a little boy that they named Asher who arrived one week after Riya. They are best friends and practically twins. They are often mistaken for twins, so they just roll with it at this point.

A few months after they were born, we collectively decided to start fresh somewhere else. We talked about it for weeks until we ended up selling everything and moving to Colorado. It's much more quaint and idyllic out here in the mountains than in Vegas.

Even after ten years, I still have nightmares of Nikolai's murder. That has been what stuck with me the longest. It plays in my head just as vividly as it did the day it happened. I go to therapy twice a month and have since shortly after Riya was born. I was diagnosed with an eating disorder and complex post-traumatic stress disorder due to chronic, long-term trauma. I was put on an anti-anxiety medication that I am still on nine years later.

I still sometimes struggle with my eating habits, but ultimately, Riya is who has gotten me through the worst of it. I swore to myself that I would never let her see that part of me. I never wanted her to think that it was normal to go days without eating because life got stressful. I want her to have a positive view of her body. She already faces enough of a hassle having to explain that her Mom has two husbands and a wife and her Dad has two wives. We've never hidden our dynamic from the kids and we have raised them to never be ashamed of love.

The love I have for Elliot, Daniel, and Lana is beyond anything comprehensible and I pray that Riya and Asher find that kind of all-consuming love with someone one day. Love is love and it is beautiful in every form.

Afterword

I took a leap of faith by redeeming Nikolai in this story. I know some will disagree with my decision, but at the end of the day... Not all trauma is straight forward. Nikolai was a bad man who did bad things to Maya. She never forgot the trauma he caused, but she was also understanding of the fact that when faced with a decision to do the right thing he did it without hesitiation. He knew he was not deserving of her forgiveness, but he still did the right thing by saving her. Doing that, means she survived and so did her little girl. Despite the trauma, acknowledging his sacrifice was an important decision I wanted her to make.

I do feel that there are people who have done heinous things that are still redeemable, so long as their heart is in the right place. Forgiveness and moving on is for your healing. Not for the one who hurt you or have an opinion of how you should heal. Forgiving someone does not have to mean forgetting what they did to you. Everyone heals from their trauma differently and there is no correct way to heal.

About The Author

Emily Klepp

Emily Klepp is a Western North Carolina native residing in eastern Tennessee with her loving husband and two beautiful children. She has been writing since she was fourteen years old as a way to cope with her anxiety. She hopes to help others be able to speak their truth by writing about topics that are considered too taboo for societal norms.

Books By This Author

Inheritance of Misfortune (book 1)
https://amazon.com/dp/B0C4575439

Misfortune of Recurrence (Book 2)
https://amazon.com/dp/B0CKSDV1YS

Broken Pieces (Book 1)
https://amazon.com/dp/B0C8FL76FC

Shattered remains (Book 2)
https://amazon.com/dp/B0CKSBTXWG

A Touch of Clarity (Book 1)
https://amazon.com/dp/B0CCPNB77X

A Touch Of Chaos (Book 2)
https://www.amazon.com/dp/B0CNZSJG7J

A Touch Of Closure (Book 3)
https://www.amazon.com/dp/B0CNZTRRLB

Indifferent Obsessions
https://amazon.com/dp/B0CGQRY2RY

Dark Prey
https://amazon.com/dp/B0CBLLTZK1

Chance Encounters
https://amazon.com/dp/B0CJDMSZ8D

Chasing freedom
https://amazon.com/dp/B0CGVTJT7N

Saving Lily
https://www.amazon.com/dp/B0CK8F4Q4C

Under Their Protection
https://amazon.com/dp/B0CKVLQFYK

Black Lace Secret
https://www.amazon.com/dp/B0CLKYF5QY

Bound by Fear
https://amazon.com/dp/B0CL52B3MC

The Ties That Bind Us
https://amazon.com/dp/B0CM35XNY5

The Fated
https://www.amazon.com/dp/B0CLKVVYDV

Escaping Shadows
https://www.amazon.com/dp/B0CN67FNSM

Beneath The Surface
https://www.amazon.com/dp/B0CN67F244

Liberated
https://www.amazon.com/dp/B0CNQDTHBK

Precious Possessions: A Dark Mafia Romance
https://www.amazon.com/dp/B0CNQT2SWW

Unshackled
https://www.amazon.com/dp/B0CNYNQL9D

Field Of Desires
https://www.amazon.com/dp/B0CNQDTHBK

Sweet Dreams
https://www.amazon.com/dp/B0CNYS5T23

Bonded To The Blood King: A Dark Fantasy Novella
https://a.co/d/70T31Gy

From Friendship To Forever
https://www.amazon.com/dp/B0CQH6584H

The Dark Side Of Love: A Dark Irish Mob Romance
https://www.amazon.com/dp/B0CQJRHGYS

Fragments Of Me
https://www.amazon.com/dp/B0CQQV63KH

Whipped Dreams
https://www.amazon.com/dp/B0CR749QT8

Masked Desires
https://www.amazon.com/dp/B0CR8Y7YPD

How To Contact The Author

1. Follow me on Facebook at facebook.com/edknovels

2. TikTok @edknovels.com

3. Instagram.com/edknovels

4. Edknovels.com

5. Join my reader group (Emily Klepp's Soon To Be Banned Book Club) at facebook.com/groups/816704736923758

6. Email me at edknovels@gmail.com

Made in the USA
Monee, IL
11 October 2024

67534477R00132